Summer holidays are SOOOOOOOOOOO boring – just kicking balls, video games and card trading. There's no homework! No bell! No school lunches! (Our school has the best broccoli.) No timetable! No Miss Morris to teach me about punctuation. (She would say there are too many exclamation marks in the last paragraph).

ROSIE AND I CAUGHT A NEWT IN THE POND AND TOOK IT HOME. THE CAT ATE IT.

3

My friends don't feel the same.

Tom looks like he's going to his hamster's funeral,

Evie looks like she ate a sock,

A MUMMY ATE
MY HOMEWORK!

A TIME-TRAVEL ADVENTURE BY
THIAGO DE MORAES

SCHOLASTIC

TO THE SQUIRRELS, AND ALL THE KIDS AT TELFERSCOT SCHOOL

PUBLISHED IN THE UK BY SCHOLASTIC CHILDREN'S BOOKS, 2020
EUSTON HOUSE, 24 EVERSHOLT STREET, LONDON, NW1 1DB, UK
A DIVISION OF SCHOLASTIC LIMITED.

LONDON   NEW YORK   TORONTO   SYDNEY   AUCKLAND
MEXICO CITY   NEW DELHI   HONG KONG

SCHOLASTIC AND ASSOCIATED LOGOS ARE TRADEMARKS AND/OR
REGISTERED TRADEMARKS OF SCHOLASTIC INC.

TEXT AND ILLUSTRATIONS © THIAGO DE MORAES, 2020

THE RIGHT OF THIAGO DE MORAES TO BE IDENTIFIED AS
THE AUTHOR AND ILLUSTRATOR OF THIS WORK HAS BEEN ASSERTED BY
HIM UNDER THE COPYRIGHT, DESIGNS AND PATENTS ACT 1988.

ISBN 978 1407 19492 9

A CIP CATALOGUE RECORD FOR THIS BOOK IS AVAILABLE FROM THE BRITISH LIBRARY.

PRINTED IN CHINA.

1 3 5 7 9 10 8 6 4 2

THIS IS A WORK OF FICTION. NAMES, CHARACTERS, PLACES, INCIDENTS
AND DIALOGUES ARE PRODUCTS OF THE AUTHOR'S IMAGINATION OR ARE USED
CTITIOUSLY. ANY RESEMBLANCE TO ACTUAL PEOPLE, LIVING OR DEAD,
EVENTS OR LOCALES IS ENTIRELY COINCIDENTAL.

WWW.SCHOLASTIC.CO.UK

MIX
Paper from
responsible sources
FSC® C008047

1

SUNDAY, SEPTEMBER 3

Tomorrow will be the best day ever. Why? Because I will finally get to go back to school!! *YAY!!*

MY HOLIDAYS WEREN'T ALL BAD...

I GOT 438 CHUBBY BLOBS CARDS THIS SUMMER. 374 WERE DOUBLES.

"UPSET ARMADILLOS" IS MY FAVOURITE VIDEO GAME - IM STILL ON LEVEL 1, BUT IT'S PRETTY TRICKY.

I know most eleven-year-olds wouldn't feel that way, but I don't know **WHY**.

Don't get me wrong, holidays can be fun, but **NOTHING** is more fun than school.

and Ryan has been silent for two whole days.

Anyway, like I said, I am happy. So tonight I'm going to have a bath, brush my teeth and go to bed early so I can be rested for tomorrow.

I wonder if Mum will let me sleep in my uniform…

MONDAY, SEPTEMBER 4

FIRST DAY BACK AT SCHOOL!

I woke up extra early and put my uniform on (Mum did not let me sleep in it). I aligned the creases on my shorts, made sure my shirt was tucked in and my socks were level. I put on my badges (Quiz Champion, Class Representative, Recycling Officer, Head Library Helper) and went down for breakfast, where I ate some toast very carefully, so as not to get crumbs on my uniform.

After breakfast, Mum, Dad and my sister Rosie walked me to school. Rosie is three. At Happy Cubs Day Nursery, she leads a band of feral toddlers who spread terror through the whole neighbourhood. Normally they terrify me too, but not today. Today I was too excited.

I said goodbye quickly. I wanted to be first through the gates so that I'd be right at the front of the year six line. Mum says that I don't always have to be at the front of every line, but I don't agree.

My friends looked even less happy today.

Tom's hamster-funeral face had developed into a global hamster-apocalypse face. Evie just grunted when I said hi. Ryan gave me a hug. A completely silent hug. That's three days now without speaking.

Our new teacher, Mr Borderman, arrived. He told me he was glad to see that at least one student seemed happy to be back at school. Then he said the first class of the day would be maths. I couldn't believe it!

My favourite. I couldn't wait to show him all the extra maths I'd been practising this holiday – it's a kind of maths called calculus and it's very advanced. Non-curricular, even.

As we walked into the classroom, Tony hit Alex on the head with his bag.

When we got to maths class, I told Mr Borderman about all the calculus I'd been learning. He said he was going to write an extra-tricky equation on the board for me to solve. I was pretty excited. What he wrote down was more complicated than anything else I'd done so far, but I wanted to give it a try.

I worked on it while everyone else did some

normal, not-so-advanced maths. It took me a while, but eventually I thought I had cracked it. I picked up the pen to write down the answer.

That's when everything went wrong.

Seriously, majorly, incredibly wrong.

What usually happens when you write the answer to a maths problem is this: you stop writing and put your pen down, then the teacher tells you whether you've got it right or not.

Well.

What doesn't usually happen is what happened next.

As I wrote the last few numbers of my answer, the

board started to vibrate and hum (it's definitely not supposed to do that). A tiny black dot appeared in the middle of the air; it hovered for a bit and then grew into a **HUGE** black hole, which filled the whole wall all the way up to the ceiling. It looked like an inside-out tornado, swirling incredibly fast and sucking all the air from the room.

There were pens, papers and schoolbags flying all around. I tried to hold on to Mr Borderman's desk, but the pull of the hole was too strong. My fingers slipped from the desk and I flew so fast through the air that I was sucked into the swirling black tornado before I even had time to scream.

WENT PITCH BLACK AND I PASSED OUT...

No idea when,
no idea where.

I woke up, face
down, in a huge
pile of sand.

I didn't know
what was going on. At
first I thought I must have
bumped my head playing football
at school, then I remembered I don't play football. It's
at the same time as chess club.

Then I remembered the huge, swirling hole that had
appeared on the board...

I curled into a ball in the sand and stayed like that
for a while. It didn't seem to help much, so I
thought it might, perhaps, be a good idea
to find out where I was.

Maybe it was a really big
sandpit?

I sat up and looked around.

I was definitely not in a sandpit. To begin with, there were no buildings anywhere. And also no roads, people, cars – not even plants. All I could see in front of me was sand.

I looked left.

SAND.

Right.

SAND.

Behind me.

SAND.

So, basically, sand.

This was far from ideal, but I wasn't going to panic (right now, that is; I might panic later).

I remembered watching a TV show with an explorer who explained how someone could survive in the wilderness. She said that, when lost in the wild, a person should ask the following questions:

1
WHERE AM I?

2
DO I HAVE ANY FOOD, TOOLS, MAPS OR USEFUL GEAR?

3
WHERE IS THE NEAREST RIVER?

4
CAN I FOLLOW THE RIVER'S COURSE? (MOST TOWNS AND CITIES ARE BUILT NEAR RIVERS, APPARENTLY.)

That all seemed pretty sensible, so I decided to give it a go.

1 - WHERE AM I?

I didn't think there were any deserts in Britain. Maybe I was in Spain. I went there on holiday with my family once; it was very hot and very sandy. If this was Spain, I was pretty sure I could find my way back home using the Spanish I'd learnt on holiday.

2 - DO I HAVE ANY TOOLS, MAPS OR USEFUL GEAR?

I checked my pockets. I had a chocolate bar, two pounds and twenty pence, my diary and a few pens (I was pretty sure the chocolate bar had been there since the last time I wore these shorts, three months ago).

3 - WHERE IS THE NEAREST RIVER?

This was the biggest problem so far. The place looked like a desert and I couldn't see a river anywhere.

4 - FOLLOWING THE RIVER

Also a bit of a problem (see answer No. 3).

I couldn't think of any more survival tips, but sitting around wasn't going to help. So I got up and started walking.

It was **INCREDIBLY** hot, which I guess made sense what with it being a desert and all. I don't think I ever felt hotter, not even when I had to dress as a woolly mammoth for a play about evolution in year three at school. After walking for just a few minutes I was covered in sweat and out of breath.

I sat down to have a rest on top of a dune. It was very quiet, but I could hear a tiny whining noise in the distance. It turned into a really loud whizzing noise.

That's when something hit me **VERY** hard on the head.

And everything went black again.

Still no idea when, still no idea where.

I opened my eyes (again). This time my head really hurt.

I tried to get up, but I didn't get very far. Probably because I'd been tied up from head to toe with a massive rope.

I heard a noise and looked up. There were people standing over me. On the one hand, that was great because it meant I wasn't alone in the Spanish desert any more.

On the other hand, their expressions weren't exactly friendly.

They were kids, just like the kids at school, but, UNLIKE the kids at school

they had shaved heads and weren't wearing trousers, dresses or shoes – just small white skirts around their waists. The thing that made me nervous was that they carried weapons. Not toy weapons, but proper, serious ones, shiny, pointy and sharp.

There were also a few dogs and a huge monkey. They looked even less friendly.

I thought that disappearing from school into a giant black hole and waking up in the desert was the worst thing to happen to me that day. I was clearly wrong.

VERY WRONG.

The kids just stood there and glared at me, which I thought was a bit rude. They were probably just waiting to see if I was friendly or not. I decided to unleash my best Spanish.

HOLA FRIENDS, ME LLAMO HENRY. ME ENCANTAN LAS ENPANADAS?

SILENCE STRANGE CHILD! STOP YOUR MINDLESS GIBBERISH,

shouted the biggest boy, whose hair was in a long plait. The monkey moved a bit closer and bared its fangs. I didn't even know that monkeys had fangs.

I thought that was a bit harsh. My Spanish is not that bad.

And that was when I realized something. The boy had spoken in a language that didn't sound anything like English, but I had understood it perfectly.

If I understood them, maybe they would understand me.

"Er... Hey!" I said, still somehow speaking the strange language. "Where am I?" I asked.

No one said a word.

"Go get father," said the boy with the plait. Another kid ran off down the dune.

"Is this Spain?" I asked.

"Spain?" the big kid said. "I don't know anywhere called 'Spain'. We are in Kemet, just outside Waset, the greatest city in the world."

I had no idea where Kemet or Waset were, which is odd because I'm very good at geography. Maybe this was a very small country, like Lichtenstein or the French Guiana.

"Can I use your phone to call my parents?" I asked the boy.

"What is a 'phone'?" he said.

"A phone, you know," I said. "The thing you use to talk to people who are far away, play games, watch videos, all that stuff."

They all looked at each other and then back at me as if I was completely insane. Which was funny, because they were the ones who didn't know what a phone was. That is insane.

THERE WAS A LION TOO.
IN RETROSPECT THE LION
SHOULD HAVE BEEN A SIGN
THINGS WEREN'T GOING
TO BE TOO EASY...

I sighed. These kids weren't much help. I would just have to wait for a grown-up to show up.

Just then, **LOADS** of grown-ups showed up. Like the kids, they weren't your regular grown-ups.

First came some guys waving huge fans made of feathers, behind them there were lots of other people wearing leopard skins and holding little smoking bowls, then some big fellas with massive swords, and finally a man arrived, wearing a huge, shiny blue and gold hat. The hat was sort of familiar. I thought I'd seen something like it on our last class museum trip.

It looked like an … Ancient Egyptian pharaoh's crown.

DEFINITELY NOT A NORMAL HAT.

SHOULD KIDS CARRY SHARP SPEARS? NO, THEY SHOULDN'T.

Wait.

It couldn't be. Could it?

LOTS OF SAND

REALLY HOT

NOT A PAIR OF SHOES OR
TROUSERS IN SIGHT

NO ONE KNOWS
WHERE SPAIN IS

NO ONE KNOWS
WHAT A PHONE IS

EVERYONE SPEAKS
A VERY DIFFERENT
LANGUAGE

THERE'S A MAN DRESSED
LIKE A PHARAOH

Maybe … I wasn't in Spain after all.

Maybe … I was in Egypt. And not just Egypt but …

ANCIENT EGYPT.

Getting back home had suddenly become a whole lot trickier.

I was trying to take all of this in when one of the leopard fur-wearing men (I don't believe people should wear real animal fur by the way; if you're cold just buy a woolly jumper, don't kill a big cat) shouted:

"Bow in the presence of the most exalted king, ruler of Kemet, renewer of the crown, strong-armed vanquisher of the nine bows, dear to Ra, beloved of Ptah…"

The pharaoh guy interrupted with a wave:

"It's OK, Paser," he said. "You don't have to do the whole thing."

"… Seti the first!" finished the leopard man, looking a bit miffed.

Everyone kneeled on the floor really fast; only the pharaoh remained standing.

He looked at me with an odd expression. I looked back (hopefully with less of an odd expression), and then I realized I was the only non-pharaoh person still standing up.

I knelt down as fast as I could, toppled over and fell face down in the sand. The big boy laughed, but the pharaoh shushed him.

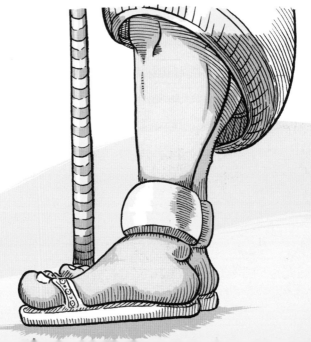

"Who are you, strange child of the desert?" Seti asked.

"I'm not from the desert, sir, I'm from Surrey," I said. "And my name is Henry."

"He-Ne-Re, from Su-Wa-Ri," said the pharaoh. "Why are you here?"

I thought about telling him the truth, but I wasn't exactly sure what that was.

"I'm, er ... lost," I said, which at least was definitely true.

The pharaoh looked at me without blinking.

Then he said:

"He-Ne-Re of Su-Wa-Ri, your name is uncommon, your appearance bizarre, your manners non-existent. You are clearly from beyond the reaches of civilization."

The kids all smirked.

"We shall bring you back to the palace," Seti said. "We need more time to decide what to do with you. Until then you are under the Crown's protection."

I didn't
like being called
bizarre, Henry is
actually a super-
popular name, my
manners are excellent
(my gran always says so),
and Surrey is very much part of
civilization, thank you. Still, going
to the palace seemed much
better than standing there in
the desert all tied up, so I
said, "Thanks," they
untied me and
I got up.

As we walked down the dune, the baboon threw a piece of fruit at my head.

We climbed into some fancy chariots and drove off. The chariots looked really nice – they were painted with golden wings and all sorts of shiny colours – but they were a lot more rickety than a car, and clearly had not been built with health and safety in mind.

There were no seatbelts (or seats), no doors, no roof,

just a wooden floor and some handles on the sides. They also went really, **REALLY** fast, and the sand was pretty uneven, so I was being bumped up and down (and in and out) of the chariots the whole time.

I spent the whole ride clinging to the handles and trying to not die horribly. I might have screamed once or twice (or twenty or thirty times, who was counting?), but it was so noisy I'm sure no one heard.

3

After a long time, bumping and shaking we reached a dirt road, and the drive became a bit smoother. The road widened, and some bushes and palm trees appeared; I could see little villages to the side, and some buildings in the distance.

As we got closer I saw the buildings were part of a big city. We rode towards it, down an avenue lined with hundreds of really cool sphinx statues, until we arrived at the foot of a huge wall. In the middle there was a massive gate, at least four storeys tall, and on its sides stood two enormous statues of a chap who looked a lot like the pharaoh, but more good-looking.

In all the books about Ancient Egypt, everything

  36

looks like it's made out of polished stone or white marble. This wasn't like that at all.

Everything – the sphinxes, the walls, the statues, even the gate – was painted in bright colours and covered in little drawings.

The gates opened and we drove in.

The city was **COMPLETELY CRAZY**. The main road looked like our local high street on the weekend before Christmas, but way busier and noisier.

There were little stalls selling all sorts of things. Dogs, cats, goats, horses, cows and monkeys were everywhere.

And there were thousands of people, all hurrying about. There wasn't a pair of trousers in sight. The

smaller kids were completely naked – I hope they weren't uncomfortable, what with all that sand.

I must've looked really odd to them, wearing my school cardigan, shorts and socks (all a bit crumpled now), but then I remembered some of the men in front of me were wearing dead leopards. You can't be shocked by shorts after seeing someone wearing a whole dead leopard.

As we rode into town, everyone stopped doing whatever they were doing, lined up in front of the buildings and started cheering for the pharaoh.

Seti waved at the crowd from his chariot, and so did the boy with the long plait. I tried to wave but almost fell off the chariot again. Tricky things, chariots.

Eventually we drove into the courtyard of a huge palace. It was surrounded by lots more statues that looked like extra-handsome pharaohs (it seems to be a common feature in statues of people that command big empires).

We got off the chariots and Seti, the pharaoh, came over. He spoke to one of the leopard dudes:

"Paser, I want you to look after He-Ne-Re. He will sleep in the prince's quarters and go the prince's school with Usermaatre and my other children. Make sure his disgusting rags are taken away and burned, and that he is bathed and dressed in appropriate clothing."

UH-OH. Mum and Dad go mad if I get as much as a drop of ketchup on my school uniform. They won't be happy about the whole thing getting burned.

The man the pharaoh had spoken to turned to me.

CHILD,
I AM PASER,
GUARDIAN OF THE ROYAL
CHAMBER, CHIEF MINISTER TO
THE KING, HIGH PRIEST OF RA,
WATCHER OF THE SACRED
RIVER. I AM ALSO IN CHARGE
OF THE PRINCE'S
EDUCATION.

Wow, that was a lot of jobs for one person. I was about to say something when the big kid wearing the plait interrupted.

"I don't see why this strange..." he started saying, but the pharaoh raised his hand and the boy stopped.

"Be quiet when your father speaks, Usermaatre," he said. The boy didn't like it, but he didn't say anything either. "You will behave as befits the son of a god and treat our guest likewise."

"Yes, Father," said the boy. He didn't look happy.

Paser (who seemed to do all the work whilst the pharaoh did all the talking) led us into the palace, through lots of corridors covered in expensive carpet and, that's right, yet more statues of the pharaoh. We arrived in a massive room, the size of a tennis court. There was no

ceiling, just some long, white curtains hanging from up high. There were trees and flowers everywhere, and lots of people were working, dusting, preparing beds and carrying fresh linen clothes. Everything looked really clean and tidy, the opposite of what a kid's bedroom usually looks like. (My bedroom is, of course, spotless.)

The big boy turned to me. He did not look particularly friendly

NORMAL, WELL-ADJUSTED 12-YEAR-OLD

FRIENDLY EYES

SENSIBLE HAIRSTYLE

REGULAR, NON-CREEPY SMILE

BACKPACK FULL OF SCHOOL MATERIAL

BOOKS

CLEAN, WELL-IRONED SCHOOL UNIFORM, INCLUDING SHORTS

UNDOMESTICATED SIBLING

SHOES

Perhaps this would be a good time to point out a few small differences between Usermaatre and I.

COMPLETELY SPOILED
TOTALLY INSANE
EGYPTIAN PRINCE

SHAVED HEAD

MANIC, TERRIFYING EYES

CREEPY SMILE

COMPLETELY AGE-INAPPROPRIATE WEAPON

LONG BRAIDS

GOLD JEWELLERY (A LOT OF IT)

WRAP (NO PANTS)

SANDALS

SORT-OF DOMESTICATED BABOON

THE BOY JUST STARED AT ME WITHOUT BLINKING.

IT WAS A BIT ODD.

IS THERE A PROBLEM?

YOU. YOU'RE A DEVIOUS SPY AND SHOULDN'T BE HERE.

OH, IS THAT IT? AND WHAT MAKES YOU THINK I WANT TO BE HERE, IN A STINKY DESERT BEING SHOUTED AT BY A RUDE IDIOT WHOSE NAME SOUNDS LIKE "USED MATTRESS"?!?

AAAAAAAAAAAGH!

I'M SORRY ABOUT UZZY. HE GETS A BIT WORKED-UP SOMETIMES, BUT HE'S OK ONCE YOU GET TO KNOW HIM.

ER... THANKS. NO WORRIES.

MY NAME IS TIA. I'M UZZY'S SISTER. GOOD TO MEET YOU HE-NE-RE.

GOOD TO MEET YOU TOO. THANKS FOR THE RESCUE.

IT'S NOTHING, I SPEND MY DAYS SAVING PEOPLE FROM UZZY. COME ON, LET'S GET SOMETHING TO EAT, YOU MUST BE HUNGRY.

What with everything that had happened, I hadn't realized the last thing I had eaten was breakfast early that morning (and three thousand years in the future).

Despite feeling incredibly hungry, I wasn't looking forward to Ancient Egyptian food. Everyone knows tasty food was invented in in the 1980s, and before that everyone ate liver and overcooked vegetables. The food

YUMMY

BREAD (BUT WATCH OUT FOR THE ODD STONE)
CHEESE (STINKY, NOT IN A GOOD WAY)
EGGS
BUTTER   FISH
FRUIT   ROAST GOOSE

in proper ancient times was probably going to be even worse than in the ancient times of my parents.

I couldn't have been more wrong.

We walked to another room, where people were bringing in little tables covered with food. Everything smelled delicious and looked reasonably normal, and I couldn't wait to get started. Tia talked me through it all.

LESS YUMMY

RAW ONIONS
UNCOOKED RANDOM
VEGETABLES
GARLIC. ALL THE GARLIC EVER
PRODUCED BY MANKIND EVER.

TOTALLY
UNACCEPTABLE

ROAST HYENA
GRUBS
BEER (WHAT THE HECK?)

I ate a lot. The hardest bit was having to drink beer, which made me feel dizzy. Tia explained the water from the Nile made people really sick, so they drank beer instead. It tasted like someone made soup out of dirty pants and then blended it with flat soda. I never thought I'd miss water so much.

After dinner someone gave me a skirt and some sandals to wear. They were quite comfortable, but a bit … airy. There's a reason why pants are so popular in the future.

We went back to the big room, where everyone apparently sleeps together. Back home I share a room with my sister Rosie, and I thought that was bad enough, but now I had to sleep next to that murderous imbecile Uzzy. Still, I was very tired. I would figure out a way to get back home tomorrow.

Tia showed me to an empty bed. It was made of hard reeds, which didn't look nearly as comfortable as my bed back home, but it was definitely better than the desert floor. I curled up and was soon fast asleep.

I woke up with a **GASP**. Something was on my chest.

Something heavy and cold and … snoring.

I stayed very, very still (I was quite impressed with myself) and tried to turn my head to see what it was.

An eye opened right in front of my face. It was very big, green and seemed to have a lot more lids than a normal eye. It also had a thin, wedge-shaped pupil.

By now I had stopped feeling surprised when horrible things happened.

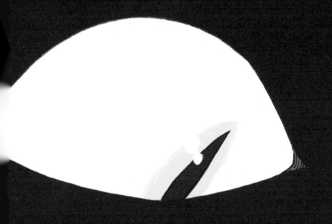

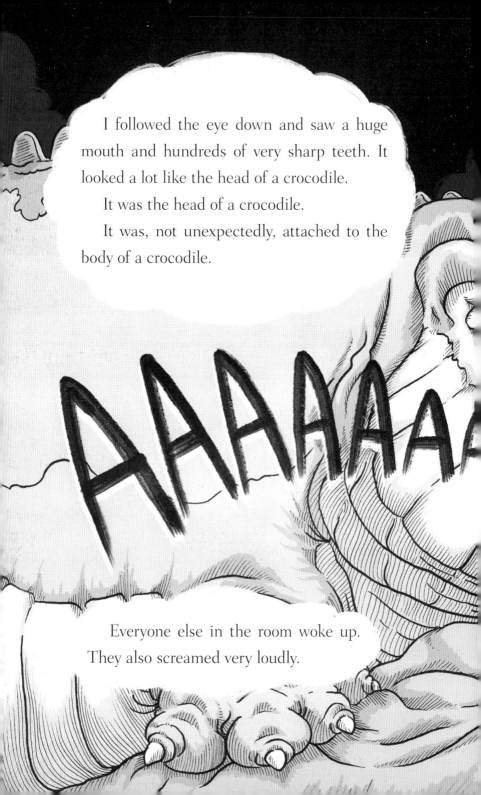

I followed the eye down and saw a huge mouth and hundreds of very sharp teeth. It looked a lot like the head of a crocodile.

It was the head of a crocodile.

It was, not unexpectedly, attached to the body of a crocodile.

AAAAAA

Everyone else in the room woke up. They also screamed very loudly.

Tia ran over. "'What happened?!?" she asked. "Are you OK?"

"It's ... it's ... it's..." I stammered, *"IT'S A MASSIVE TOOTHY CROCODILE!!!!!"*

The crocodile looked a bit offended by that and, oddly, so did Tia.

"Of course it's a crocodile, silly," she said, not looking too impressed. "It's my crocodile, Sobby, and

he was just cuddling up with you. I wondered where he was."

"YOUR CROCODILE?!?!" I asked. She nodded.

"Cuddling up? CUDDLING UP?!?! The horrid thing was going to eat me!" I said.

"That's ridiculous." she said. "Sobby is a lovely pet, and I would like you to apologize to him right now for calling him horrid and toothy. He is very sensitive about the way his teeth look."

Well, they say there's always a first time for everything, and my time to apologize to a huge reptile had arrived.

"Er... Sorry, Sobby," I said. Sobby didn't look too impressed. "I shouldn't have called you 'toothy'. Your smile is lovely."

Sobby seemed to accept my apology; at any rate, he turned around and went back to sleep. Everyone else went back to bed and I was left there in the dark, fully awake, totally pantsless, next to biggest animal I had ever seen outside a zoo.

NO IDEA WHEN,
WASET, ANCIENT EGYPT

I woke up the next morning with the sun shining into the room. For a moment I thought I was back at home in my bed.

It didn't take me long to remember what had happened, though. At least I had survived the night.

I wanted to find Tia, who seemed to be the only sane person in the whole place. She wasn't there, and neither was Uzzy, but a boy called Hano came over and introduced himself. He looked different to the other kids – his hair hadn't been shaven and he wasn't wearing jewellery. He told me he worked at the palace.

Hano brought me some breakfast. It seemed to consist mainly of huge raw onions, and since everyone else was munching theirs happily enough, I figured it wasn't a prank, just a terrible gastronomical choice.

If I ever made it back home, I'd never complain about porridge again.

"All of the pharaoh's children go to a special school here in the palace," Hano said. "It's just down the corridor from here, come on."

I was going to complain that I hadn't even had time to brush my teeth when it occurred to me they had no toothbrushes or toothpaste this far in the past. Proper oral hygiene, there was another thing to put on a list of "things to invent", right next to pants.

I followed Hano and we arrived in another big room full of kids of all ages. Tia was there already, and she introduced me to some of the other kids that went to the Prince's School. Being the new guy (a few thousand years new, in my case) is not easy, so I asked Tia to tell me who the other students were, and I made sure to take notes.

PRINCE'S SCHOOL
WASET, CLASS OF 1291 BC

USERMAATRE (UZZY)
CROWN PRINCE, BULLY
AND ALL-ROUND MASSIVE
TURNIP. ENJOYS HITTING
THINGS VERY HARD
AND BEING FIRST AT
EVERYTHING. NOT MY
FAVOURITE HUMAN BEING.

MERYATUM (MERRY)
ANOTHER ONE OF THE
PHARAOH'S KIDS. VERY
QUIET AND, DESPITE HIS
NICKNAME, A BIT GRUMPY,
PROBABLY ON ACCOUNT
OF HAVING SPENT HIS
WHOLE LIFE AROUND UZZY

KNEB
SON OF A REALLY
IMPORTANT SCRIBE
THAT'S A PERSON
WHO WRITES THINGS
DOWN (IT'S QUITE
AN IMPORTANT JOB,
APPARENTLY). QUITE
NICE, SPENDS ALL HIS
TIME DOODLING IN CLASS
(WHICH IS LESS OF A
PROBLEM IN ANCIENT
EGYPT THAN IN THE 21ST
CENTURY, BECAUSE
THEIR WRITING IS LOTS
OF LITTLE DOODLES
ANYWAY).

TIA
UZZY'S SISTER AND MY
FIRST (AND ONLY) ANCIENT
EGYPTIAN FRIEND.
APPARENTLY GIRLS ARE
NOT ALLOWED TO LEARN
HOW TO READ OR WRITE
IN ANCIENT EGYPT, WHICH
SEEMS PRETTY TERRIBLE,
BUT TIA COMES TO
SCHOOL ANYWAY. I DON'T
THINK ANYONE HAS THE
COURAGE TO TELL HER
NOT TO.

NEBCHASETNEBET (NEBBY)
LIZZY AND TIA'S BROTHER. HASN'T TRIED TO KILL ME YET, SO SEEMS LIKE A REASONABLY DECENT CHAP. BROUGHT A SNAKE TO SCHOOL.

DEDU
DEDU'S DAD IS AN ARCHITECT. AN ARCHITECT IS SOMEONE WHO DESIGNS BUILDINGS AND HE'S DONE LOADS FOR THE PHARAOH.

HANO
I HADN'T UNDERSTOOD WHEN WE MET, BUT HANO IS A SLAVE. THAT MEANS THAT THE PHARAOH OWNS HIM, LIKE SOMEONE OWNS A PAIR OF TRAINERS OR A BICYCLE, WHICH SEEMS ... NOT RIGHT. EXTREMELY NOT RIGHT. HANO HAS TO WORK ALL DAY, EVERY DAY, WITHOUT GETTING PAID. IT'S HOW THINGS ARE IN ANCIENT EGYPT BUT IT SEEMS RUBBISH. EVERYONE LIKES HIM, AND HE SEEMS TO HAVE FOUND A WAY TO SNEAK INTO SCHOOL.

NEFERTARI (NEFFY)
TIA'S BEST FRIEND, ANOTHER GIRL WHO IS NOT SUPPOSED TO BE AT SCHOOL, BUT IS. NOT THE FRIENDLIEST PERSON I'VE MET (SHE GRUNTED WHEN I SAID "HELLO" THEN MOVED TO THE OPPOSITE SIDE OF THE ROOM FROM ME).

ME
HE-NE-RE OF SU-WA-RI (MUST TEACH PEOPLE HOW TO PRONOUNCE MY NAME PROPERLY).

Being back in a classroom made me feel a bit happier. I might have been three thousand years in the past, but this was school. I'm good at school. **AMAZING** at it, in fact. I knew what I was doing with school.

We waited for the teacher. A man walked through the door. A really big man. His arm muscles were so big that it looked like he had hidden some coconuts inside them. Maybe he was the teacher's bodyguard or something. He looked at me.

"**WHAT ARE YOU DOING SITTING THERE?!?!**" he yelled. I noticed everyone else was standing. "Up with you! Everyone jogging to the field, right now! Hup-Hup! **OFF YOU GO, YOU BUNCH OF DESERT RATS!**"

I guess he was the teacher. Perhaps they started the day with a PE lesson. I didn't mind PE too much – I had been on the netball team back at school until it got in the way of extra maths.

We jogged out of the room, through some gardens and into a big dusty field. I noticed that instead of balls the teacher seemed to be carrying a bundle of long sticks with sharp metal bits at the end.

Odd.

"**ALL RIGHT, POND TOADS,**" he yelled. "Today we're learning about spears. Handling, stabbing, parrying. I want everyone in a line. **NOW!**"

I didn't like the sound of "spears" or "stabbing" too much.

The teacher started handing spears to all the kids in the line. They were very heavy and very sharp.

"**YOU!**" he said, pointing at me "What's your name?"

"Henry, sir," I said.

"Hen-Re-Ser? Funny name. Are you any good with

a spear?" he asked.

"We're about to find out, sir," I said, holding the pointy end of the spear as far away from me as possible.

He didn't seem too impressed.

"We don't want you dying on your first day. You can train with Kammy over there."

Kammy was standing at the end of the line. He was only two or three years old, but quite hefty. I didn't know if I should feel humiliated for being paired up with a toddler or happy I wasn't going to be skewered to death by Uzzy.

The teacher's name was Master Tchay. He showed us a few moves and told us to repeat them. Kammy and I found a corner to practise. He reminded me a bit of my sister, but holding a weapon. Not a good thing.

I was trying to figure out my spear grip when I felt a sharp pain in my knee. Kammy had just stabbed me. In fact he'd stabbed me quite hard.

I was too stunned to speak. He yelled and came for me again, twirling his spear like a tiny, chubby helicopter. I dropped my spear and ran as he chased me around the field. Kammy was very fast for someone so small. In the end, Master Tchay stepped in.

"I see that Kammy was too much for you," said
Master Tchay, not looking too pleased. Oddly, the lack
of pleasing seem to be aimed at me, not at the kid that
had been trying to kill me with a spear.

"He-Ne-Re, today you can practise by yourself," he
said.

"Kammy," he said, turning to the other boy. 'That
was very good."

"The only thing you need to watch out for is your
grip. Push with the back hand and you can get the
spear in much deeper, right?" Master Tchay put Kammy
down and ruffled his hair. "Good boy. Off you go."

As I walked back inside to clean my wound, Uzzy walked past and said, "Don't think you can fool me by pretending to be useless. I don't trust you."

These people were COMPLETE LUNATICS.

The lesson lasted the whole day. Against all probability, I managed to survive.

When we finally got back to our room, I was so tired I couldn't stand straight. I'd done nothing about trying to get back home, but I didn't know where to start, and had no energy to think about anything besides sleep.

Sobby was still curled up in my corner. I didn't even try to push him away this time, just lay down and fell asleep on top of him.

The rest of the week was more exhausting than anything I've ever gone through. It was also very long: a week in Ancient Egypt does not last seven days like our week; it lasts ten days, with two left for resting.

DAY ONE: THE ARTS OF WAR
TURNS OUT THIS WASN'T "ART" IN THE SENSE OF PAINTING OR DRAWING, JUST HOURS OF BEING HIT VERY HARD WITH ALL SORTS OF POINTY THINGS. MY SECOND CLASS IN SPEAR FIGHTING WENT MUCH BETTER. I'M PRETTY SURE MY SPEAR GRAZED SOMEONE'S TOE THIS TIME.

DAY TWO: HUNTING
IF YOU'RE RICH IN ANCIENT EGYPT YOU GO HUNTING FOR FUN, WHICH IS ODD, BECAUSE HUNTING IS NO FUN AT ALL. I HAD TO START WITH SOMETHING EASY, SO WENT FOR A TOAD. IT WASN'T EASY. IT WAS HORRIBLE. TOADS ARE A LOT MORE AGGRESSIVE THEN THEY LOOK.

DAY THREE: GEOMETRY
WE BUILT A LEVEL TO MEASURE THE ANGLE OF THINGS. MINE WASN'T EXACTLY LEVEL.

DAY FOUR: CHARIOT DRIVING
ANOTHER THING EGYPTIANS REALLY LIKE TO DO IS WHIZZ ABOUT VERY FAST ON CHARIOTS PULLED BY HORSES. LUCKILY MY HORSE WAS GOOD AT STEERING, BECAUSE I FELL OUT OF THE CHARIOT AND HAD TO HANG ON FOR LIFE FOR MOST OF THE LESSON. I GAVE THE HORSE A THANK YOU BAG OF CARROTS.

DAY FIVE: WRITING IN HIEROGLYPHS
THIS IS A LOT MORE COMPLICATED THAN NORMAL WRITING, BUT I WAS PRETTY GOOD AT IT (PLUS NO INJURIES, YAY!)

DAY SIX: POTIONS
WE WON'T TALK ABOUT POTIONS.

DAY SEVEN: RE
A REALLY OLD PRIEST READ FROM A BOOK THAT TELLS DEAD PEOPLE HOW TO BEHAVE AFTER THEY DIE. I CAN SEE WHY THEY THINK ABOUT DEATH SO MUCH, WHAT WITH THE DESERT, THE CROCODILES AND THE SPEARS.

DAY 8: ASTRONOMY
A LOT OF ANCIENT EGYPTIAN
ASTRONOMY IS, IN FACT, ASTROLOGY.
THE FIRST IS A BRANCH OF SPACE
SCIENCE, THE LATTER A HUGE
AMOUNT OF NONSENSE ABOUT STARS
CONTROLLING PEOPLE'S LIVES. TODAY
I LEARNT NEXT MONDAY WOULD BE
AN UNLUCKY DAY FOR FARMING AND
WEAVING BECAUSE THE PATTERN
OF SOME STARS LOOKS A BIT LIKE A
DANCING CRAB (IF YOU SQUINT LOTS
AND TURN YOUR HEAD SIDEWAYS).

The last two days of the week were resting days. Uzzy went out to practise sword fighting or some other murderous pastime with his friends and his baboon. Tia and I had started spending quite a bit of time together, and she invited me to go horse riding, which didn't feel restful at all, so I politely said no.

I was finally alone. And I was going to use this time to figure out how to get home. I didn't think it was going to be easy. But it must be something to do with that maths equation I had written on the board. If I could write that down again, maybe it would help me get home.

I couldn't remember what it was. Still, I had to start somewhere.

I went looking for Hano and asked him if he could help me find some paper (which over here is actually a bunch of pressed leaves called papyrus) and a pen (a reed dipped in ink) and set off to work.

I sat down by my bed, put my pen to paper (well, put my reed to papyrus) and tried to write the problem down. Trouble is, I couldn't remember anything much and the little I wrote made no sense.

I tried for **AGES**, and was starting to feel quite sorry for myself, when Hano and Tia walked in.

"What's that?" Hano said, nodding at my papyrus full of writing.

"Just some maths," I said, rolling my papyrus quickly. I wanted to tell them what I was doing, but it's not that easy to explain you have been the victim of a space/time accident.

"Doesn't look like maths to me," said Tia. She looked suspicious. "Just some funny squiggles."

"That's how we write where I come from," I said.

"Why are you all by yourself writing on a rest day?"

she asked. "Perhaps you really are a spy, like my brother says."

"NO WAY!" Hano said. "Spies are good at stuff. He's rubbish at fighting. And riding chariots. And hunting. And…"

"Thanks, Hano. We get the idea," I said.

"He could be faking all that," said Tia. She looked at me and smiled. "You'd have to be a really good spy to fake that toad attack."

"We're going into the city with the others, want to come along?" asked Hano.

I sighed. I wasn't getting anywhere with my equation. "Sure."

The garden was full of kids waiting for us. Even Uzzy's baboon Mumbles was there, giving me a distinctively EVIL look.

"Ugh," muttered Uzzy. "Why is he coming?"

"Because he's our guest and my friend," she said. "So let's go, unless you want one of the teachers to see us."

We walked down courtyards and corridors until we got to a tiny door inside a massive wall. Hano got a key out of a bag that was tied to his belt and opened the door. It led to a small, dusty alley. We were leaving the palace for the first time since I had come to Waset!

I was going to ask if we were allowed out or not, but as I opened my mouth Tia gave me a very meaningful look. I didn't understand the meaning of it, of course, but it was enough for me to be quiet and leave the questions for another time.

The little alley led up to the noisy, bustling main street we had driven through on the day I'd arrived.

"Let's go to the market," said Dedu. "I really fancy some candy."

"Oh yes," I said. "I haven't had any candy in ages. I even fancy having some kola cubes, and I hate kola cubes..."

Uzzy gave me such an unfriendly look that I fell silent.

We walked until we reached another large street. Long sheets of fabric hung from between the buildings, making the ground shady and cool (which was great, because the day was baking hot, as always).

There were hundreds of stalls everywhere, with people selling all sorts of things. A lot of it was food, but there were also statues, jewellery, clothes and pottery. One stall sold copies of the book we were reading at school (it was officially called *The Book of Going Forth By Day*, but everyone called it *The Book of the Dead*), another sold all sorts of pets. Having slept on top of Sobby for a few weeks, I wasn't surprised to see a basket full of baby crocodiles next to a box full of kittens.

Compared to the last few days, this was good fun. I should've known it wasn't going to last long.

We finally arrived at a stall that sold sweets, and Tia was buying some for everyone. They looked a lot like balls of horse poo, but Hano said they were candied date balls, and that they were delicious.

Well, anything would make a change from raw onion. I was just about to eat mine when Mumbles went bonkers, climbed over the table and started scoffing everything.

He clearly really liked date balls.

The stall holder went COMPLETELY BANANAS.

"GET YOUR MONKEY DOWN!! GET THE MONKEY DOWN!"

he yelled at us. "Why do you bring this horrendous monstrosity to a sweet stall?!?! *IT BELONGS IN CHAINS!! IN CHAINS!!*"

he shouted, even louder, waving at some guys that were standing down the road. They were very big, carried enormous swords and had two huge black dogs with them. The guards ran towards us, also shouting. By this point there were several people shouting:

Uzzy was shouting at Mumbles to stop and come down right now.

Tia and Hano were shouting at Uzzy to get a move on before the guards arrived.

The sweet stall man was shouting for help from the

other sellers.

The other sellers were shouting that they were going to catch and flog us kids (I felt that was a bit unfair – it was the baboon who was doing all the wrong stuff).

I was shouting in ABSOLUTE TERROR. Mumbles, having finished all the dates, jumped down from the stall. We ran very fast (still shouting) towards the main road. Behind us came a dozen guards, two dogs and at least fifty angry stall-holders. They were rather fast.

Finally we reached the palace door – only for Hano to drop the keys.

Mumbles swiftly leapt over the palace gate, still munching sweets.

The angry mob got closer. I had read about angry mobs in books before. This was definitely a mob, and obviously angry.

"What are we going to do?" yelped Tia. "They look like they're ready to chop us into tiny bits."

"Er … leave it to me," I said. "I believe a reasonable argument is the best way to solve a problem like this, and I am rather good at reasonable arguments…" I cleared my throat and was turning to the mob to speak when Hano yelled, *"THEY ARE GOING TO KILL US!"* and all the angry people rushed towards us.

There was a loud SNAPPING sound behind us. I turned around and saw that Uzzy had broken the lock using the tip of his (very, very sharp) knife.

"Quick, everyone through!" he shouted, pushing us past the door.

We all scrambled past as Uzzy held the door open. I turned, prepared to hold the door shut, when I realized the mob had stopped running.

They looked at us. They looked at the palace courtyard. They then became very silent, turned their backs and went away, shuffling.

It took me a while to understand what had happened. Turns out it's a lot easier to get away with doing something wrong if you're royalty. If a normal person had done what we did they would be fed to the crocodiles by now (not to Sobby, of course; turns out Sobby is a very nice pet, so he would never eat a person).

We went back to our room and had recovered from the near-death experience enough to start laughing about it, when Paser walked in. Followed by the pharaoh.

Usually it was impossible to tell which mood Seti was in, but it was pretty obvious this time.

"We are disappointed and angry," he said quietly, which sounded a lot more scary than shouting. "We would like an explanation."

I thought Uzzy was going to lie or blame the whole thing on the monkey, but he didn't.

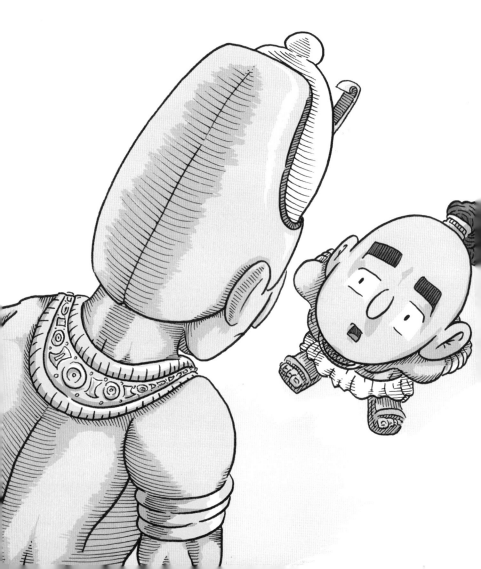

"I am sorry, father. It was all my fault," he said. "I lost control of Mumbles and he made a mess."

Uzzy is still a turnip, but that was pretty brave of him to own up to the baboon's mess. For once it hadn't been Uzzy making the trouble.

"It will not happen again, Usermaatre. You will be punished. And you," said the pharaoh, pointing at the rest of us, "since you can't control your pets, you shall not have them for a month."

He looked around at us all, then turned to go. "Paser, make sure the shopkeeper is compensated."

Seti turned around and left, followed by Uzzy. When Uzzy came back he looked really miserable, but he didn't complain or say anything about it.

Everyone missed their pets. I even found myself missing Sobby a bit. Sleeping with him was a lot more comfy than the hard bed or the floor, and his big toothy smile cheered me up.

COMPLETELY INAPPROPRIATE PETS

SOBBY
ONLY LOOKS SCARY, BUT IS A BIG SOFTY (LITERALLY, HIS BELLY IS SOOO SOFT). OCCASIONALLY EATS A FEW OF THE OTHER PETS, BUT HASN'T TRIED TO EAT ME SO FAR.

BEGBEH
HANO'S PET RAT. MUST BE VERY WELL FED, BECAUSE HE IS THE SIZE OF A SMALL DOG.

MUMBLES
WELL-KNOWN BABOON WITH VIOLENT TENDENCIES. A MASSIVE BUNDLE OF FUR, FANGS AND LACK OF MANNERS.

MR WHISKERS
MERRY'S LION. NOT A
LION CUB BUT A BIG,
GROWN-UP LION WITH A
MANE, CLAWS AND ALL THE
WORKS. ALL HE DOES IS EAT
AND SLEEP.

CUDDLES
TIA'S CAT, ALMOST AS
SCARY AND ANTI-SOCIAL
AS MUMBLES. THE SIZE OF
A SMALL SHEEP, JUMPS
ON TOP OF PEOPLE WHEN
THEY LEAST EXPECT IT.

POPPY
POPPY IS A MASSIVE
HOODED SNAKE THAT
NEBBY USES AS A SCARF.
A LOT FRIENDLIER THAN
THE CAT.

5 (I FINALLY LEARNT HOW TO WRITE ANCIENT EGYPTIAN DATES, YAY)

2ND YEAR OF THE REIGN OF SETI I,
8TH DAY OF THE 1ST MONTH OF HARVEST.

A new week began and we were back at school. I was glad, because those two rest days had definitely not been restful at all.

In the morning we had arts of war (or "hitting Henry with a large stick again") class, and that went as expected. We rested in the afternoon because the second class, astronomy, happened at night. The teacher was a small, round man called Master Heneb. He took a long time to explain everything and people kept falling asleep in his lessons, but I liked him.

There were no clocks, compasses or mobile phones with maps in Ancient Egypt, so it turns out astronomy was really important. They used the positions of stars in the night sky to figure out a lot of stuff.

"Good night, class," said Master Heneb. "Today I thought we could go through what we have learnt in these past few weeks and make sure we all understood everything, or at least something."

A mumble went through the class; besides Tia and I, no one liked astronomy class much, and they liked night-time revision even less. I was fine; I like revision at any time of the day (or night).

"These are the four main celestial charts we have," our teacher continued. "They show us where the stars are at different times at night, and that's important because…?"

I put my hand up. No one else did.

"Yes, He-Ne-Re?" said Master Heneb

"Knowing where the stars are at different times of the night is important so we can tell the time, sir," I answered. "It's easy when the sun is up, but quite tricky in the dark."

"Very good He-Ne-Re," he said. "Now, why do we look for the rise of the star called Sopdet before sunrise?"

I put my hand up again. It was only me, again.

"He-Ne-Re has already been," said the master,

looking a bit miffed. "Anyone else?"

Tia must have taken pity seeing Master Heneb's face, so she answered, "When Sopdet appears on the horizon before sunrise, the flooding season begins."

"EXACTLY!" the teacher said, breaking into a big smile. "Very good, Tia. Now, let's see who can remember the names of some of our most important constellations."

Master Heneb pointed out some constellations and told us their names. I struggled to see the shapes he told us about, so I thought I'd make up my own names:

ANCIENT EGYPTIAN
CONSTELLATIONS

THE EAGLE

THE BULL

THE CROCODILE

THE TORTOISES

THE PLOUGH

HENRY'S
(MUCH MORE REALISTIC)
CONSTELLATIONS

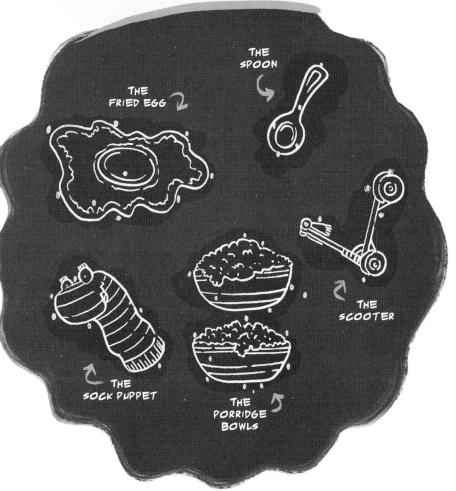

THE
SPOON

THE
FRIED EGG

THE
SCOOTER

THE
SOCK PUPPET

THE
PORRIDGE
BOWLS

The lesson got me thinking about how to use the stars to figure out the time. I was completely stuck with my plan to get back home, so I thought I might ask Master Heneb for some help. He knew a lot about maths, but also believed the stars were giant gods hanging off the night sky (which was also a goddess, probably bored to death from having people dangling from her), so it might not take much to make him believe in time travel.

After the class ended I stayed back and spoke to him.

"Master Heneb," I said, "can I ask you something?"

"Of course you can, He-Ne-Re," he said. "What is it?"

"How much do you know about time?" I asked.

"What do you mean by 'time'?" he asked. "The hours, days and months?"

"Not really…" I said. "More like how time works. Is it possible for someone to go from one day, let's say today, to another, let's say a month ago?" I asked. "To go back in time?"

He raised his eyebrows and thought for a bit.

"That's not an easy question to answer," he said.

"We think that time runs in a circle, so things happen again and again at the same times – like the flooding of the Nile or the rising of the sun. Perhaps, if you stood in the same place for long enough, you'd go through a whole cycle of time and get back to where you were at the beginning, but our lives are too short for that to happen."

"Thanks, Master Heneb," I said, rather miserably. Waiting for another **3000 YEARS** definitely did not seem like a practical solution.

He could see I wasn't happy with his answer.

"Is there something worrying you, He-Ne-Re?" he asked. "Can I help?"

I wanted to tell him everything but it sounded too crazy, even to me.

"It's just a silly idea I had," I said. "Thanks anyway."

He gave me a funny look, and I went back to my room.

I would have to solve this on my own.

Going back to the future wasn't my only worry. Our routine at the palace was so strict that occasionally we had to let off steam. Even I felt the need to behave in a not-necessarily-ideal way for the first time in my life. Here are some of the things we got up to:

LET ALL THE CHICKENS FROM THE ROYAL COOP LOOSE.

PAINTED MOUSTACHES ON THE PHARAOH'S
STATUES IN THE COURTYARD.

SWAM IN THE SACRED PALACE POND (AND WERE
ALMOST EATEN BY THE SACRED PALACE HIPPOS).

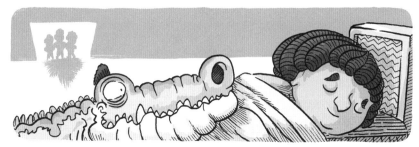

LED SOBBY INTO PASER'S BED WHEN HE WAS SLEEPING.

WROTE "ROYAL SCHOOL KIDS RULEZ"
ON THE KING'S TOILET'S WALLS

ATE ALL THE CANDIED DATES FROM THE ROYAL LARDER.

6

Paser came in this morning and told us the whole class was going to a school trip soon to visit the **VALLEY OF THE DEAD** (I hoped the name was just a figure of speech).

Everybody got really excited about the trip, even Uzzy. We hadn't been allowed to leave the palace since the incident at the sweet stall (thanks again, Mumbles).

In all the school trips I had done before (in the future, I mean), I always took the same things: a packed lunch, some water and a raincoat in case it rained. This was clearly going to be a bit different; besides us kids and the teachers (Paser and Master Tchay) we had lots of servants, guards and even a cook coming along.

We rode there on camels and I couldn't decide whether camels were more or less uncomfortable than the chariots. It was a close call so I made a list.

CAMEL

PLUSES
- GOES SLOWLY
- HAS A (NOT PARTICULARLY COMFORTABLE) SEAT

MINUSES
- IS VERY TALL
- IS HORRIBLY WOBBLY
- STINKS LIKE A PILE OF UNWASHED PANTS
- LICKS PEOPLE
- FARTS
- KEEPS GIVING ME THE EVILS
- MAKES ME VIOLENTLY SICK
- IS DRIVEN BY ME

CHARIOT

PLUSES
- IS REASONABLY CLOSE TO THE GROUND
- SMELLS OK
- DOESN'T LICK ME
- DOESN'T FART
- DOESN'T GIVE ME VICIOUS LOOKS
- IS DRIVEN BY A RESPONSIBLE ADULT

MINUSES
- GOES VERY FAST
- IS HORRIBLY WOBBLY
- THERE'S NO PLACE TO SIT

All in all, I think the chariot wins this one.

We had to leave early so the midday sun wouldn't catch us in the desert. The camels WOBBLED up and down through the city and across the river. I only fell off two or three times, and by the time we had crossed I wasn't even being sick any more (the wobbling was awful).

We arrived at the entrance of a huge temple, which seemed to have been carved into the side of a mountain. Behind the mountain were more mountains, stretching to both sides as far as I could see. There was no vegetation, just brown rock and sand.

Uzzy had a point there, but I wasn't about to agree.

The camels kneeled, we dismounted (some less elegantly than others) and sat down to have lunch. Paser explained what was going to happen.

"Behind these mountains are two valleys," he said, "where the tombs of lots of important ancient pharaohs are. Unlike the pyramids, these tombs are huge rooms cut into the stone of the mountain. As you know, a part of our soul survives after death, and it needs all possible comforts in the world of the dead. The tombs are filled with treasure, chariots, boats, food, servants, etc."

Did he say servants? It was probably better not to think too much about that...

"We will split into two groups and make our way through the tombs," he finished.

He split us into the groups. I was alongside Tia **(YAY!)** and Uzzy **(NOT YAY)**. Hano came along too, carrying snacks and sun umbrellas.

We walked through a path in the mountain until we got to the valleys. Our group went left, and Master Tchay's went right. The place was **ENORMOUS**, so after a few minutes' walking we couldn't hear the others (and they were very loud).

There were huge gates carved from the rock all

across the side of the mountain. Some had big pharaoh statues on the sides, others had really pretty carved columns and one even had a huge statue of a man with a crocodile's head that reminded me of Sobby.

Even the doors were made of rock, which wasn't too practical. We couldn't wait to go inside, so we asked Paser which one would we visit first.

"What do you mean, 'visit'?" he asked.

"Visit, you know," said Uzzy. "Go inside, look at stuff."

Paser looked really confused.

"Don't be silly, children," he said. "We can't go inside the tombs. That's where your ancestors are resting. We don't want to disturb them."

Well, that was no fun at all.

"I can't believe we came all the way here to look at a wall," said Tia. He had a point; these reasonably interesting as walls go, but they were still just walls.

"Well, Mistress Tia," Paser replied, "it's not just a wall; these carvings tell the story of the people that lie behind the doors. I suggest you children go along and learn as much as you can from them – I'll be asking questions on the way back."

He walked off to find a place to rest and left us there, staring at the closed gates.

The first gate was reasonably interesting. The carvings said that inside was king so-and-so, favourite of this god or the other, conqueror of some people somewhere. The next gate was the same, and so was the next. The only thing that seemed to change were the names. By the fourth gate even I was bored with reading the same thing over and over again.

We walked down the narrow valley in silence. After all the expectation of the trip, this was pretty disappointing. If I had pockets I would have put my hands in them.

Hano stopped.

"Guys…" he said.

"What?" I asked.

"LOOK AT THAT GATE!" he said.

"We've looked at enough gates for the day, thanks, Hano," said Uzzy.

"No! Listen to me. Look at that gate," replied Hano.

We all looked (it's not like we had something better to do). It was another massive rock gate like all the others, except that the door on this one was half open.

"LET'S GO IN!" said Uzzy, and everyone started following him. Everyone, that is, but me.

"Paser said we shouldn't," I said.

"OOOOOOOOOOH..." Uzzy said mockingly. "You always do everything you're told," he said. "Have you tried having some fun? Once in your life? Or do you always wait for someone else to tell you what to do?" **THAT WASN'T ON.**

"I have had a lot of fun in my life, thank you very much," I said. "I still remember a lovely afternoon I spent reorganizing my bookshelf in subject and alphabetical order."

Hano moved forward. He had a funny look on his face.

"He-Ne-Re, thing is ... you don't always have to do what you're told," he said. "Look at me. If I only did what I was told, I would spend all my days cleaning horse dung back at the palace stables. I wouldn't be here now, or be friends with you guys."

Uzzy smiled at him. "See? Breaking the rules can be a good thing. Come on."

"OK, fine," I said, there was little point in arguing. "Let's go."

I had agreed to go in, but that didn't mean I had to like it.

We squeezed through the gap in the door into a small chamber, with walls covered in all sorts of **AMAZING** paintings and writings. It was really dark and smelled like those dried flowers which old people

leave in the loo to make it smell nice, but doesn't. At the far end was another door – this one was wide open and led to a corridor.

The corridor was much darker than the entrance chamber. After turning a few times this way and that, the light from the outside disappeared completely and we were left in *TOTAL DARKNESS.*

I'm not afraid of the dark (maybe just a little), but being in a pitch-black corridor inside a tomb full of mummies in a huge hole carved into a mountainside in a desert wasn't helping me feel too cheery.

"Are you coming or not?" whispered Tia.

"I'm not sure we need to go in further," I said. What I meant to say was that I was absolutely sure we shouldn't go in any further. Tia wasn't impressed. "Oh, come on, He-Ne-Re, it's just a little bit dark," she said, and kept on going.

Making my way back outside on my own felt worse than staying with the others, so I just kept following them. Slowly, my eyes got used to the dark and, with a few stumbles and trips, we got to another chamber.

This room was **WAY BIGGER** than the first. It was filled with all sorts of amazing stuff. There were shelves with clothes, beer jars, a table with dishes and cutlery, two really big boats and even a golden chariot (no camel, thankfully). Apparently the Ancient Egyptians believed the kings had to take everything they needed with them to the after-life (perhaps there were no shops there).

Uzzy found a huge sword and was playing with it.

"This is fun, but I want to see a sarcophagus," he said, grinning. "Say hello to our great-great-great-granddad!"

I was about to say I wasn't too keen to get close to the desiccated body of a dead person when Tia called in a low whisper.

"**SHHHHHHH!!!!**" she said. "I think there's something moving over there."

We all stopped and looked at Tia. She was pointing at another door, on the far end of the room. It was only a little bit open but, now that we were all quiet, we could hear a noise coming through it. It sounded like someone scrunching a ball of paper very hard.

Uzzy walked over. "Come and see this," he whispered.

I definitely didn't want to come in. In fact, I wanted to talk about how it might make more sense to walk away from creepy noises in tombs, not towards them. Thing is, I was so scared I didn't want to make much noise, let alone talk.

No one else seemed that bothered, they all crossed over into the other room. I waited and, after not hearing any terrified screams, crossed over too.

On the other side was another massive room. Right in the middle there was a **HUGE** stone sarcophagus. It was made of polished grey rock, and the lid was carved with the features of a pharaoh.

Odd thing, even though this guy was hundreds of years old, the face sculpted on the lid looked a lot like Uzzy's dad. We could see the face carving well because the lid was propped up on the side of the sarcophagus.

"Er ... guys..." I whispered. "Shouldn't this lid be on top of the sarcophagus?"

"What?" said Uzzy.

"On top, you know, closing it?" I said. "Keeping the dead person inside?"

"Oh," said Uzzy. "Yeah, that is a bit odd."

EVERYONE HAD SUDDENLY BECOME VERY STILL AND VERY QUIET.

"We should leave," I squeaked.

Tia turned around to head back, and hit a bronze shield that had been hanging on the wall.

The shield fell down with a loud...

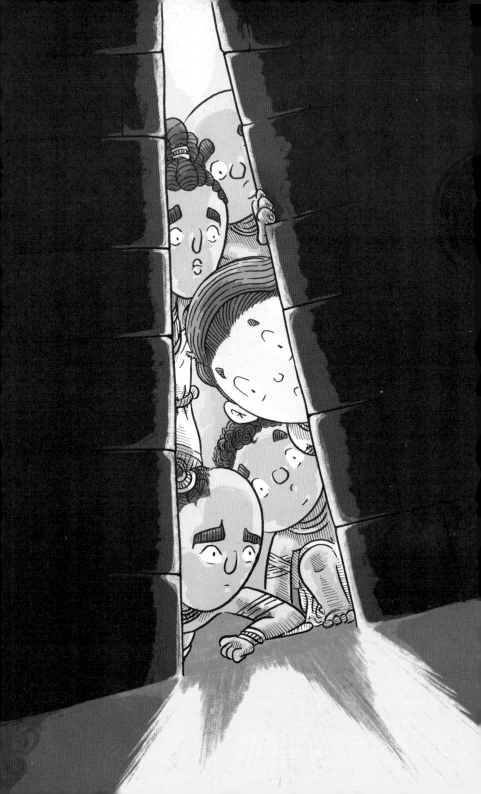

like a big bell ringing. Surprisingly loud, bronze shields.

There was silence, and in that silence we heard that same rustling sound we had heard earlier. Slowly, we all turned…

SOMETHING was coming out of the sarcophagus.

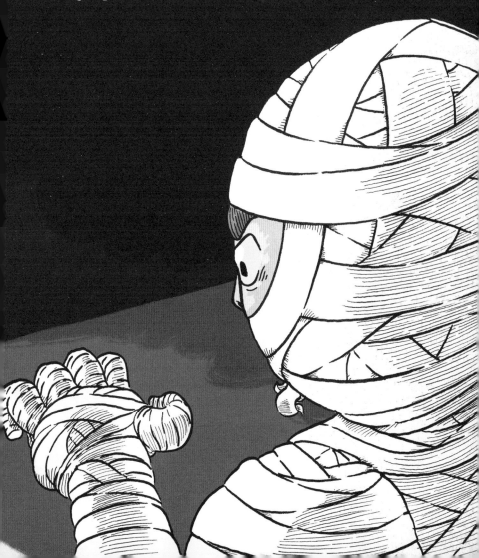

I hoped it was something harmless, like a completely new species of panda or a banjo-playing cat, but it wasn't.

It was a really big man, all covered in strips of fabric, gold and jewels. Lots of beetles came out from the gaps in between his wrappings as he made his way out of the sarcophagus.

His face was the only uncovered bit. It was grey and blotchy, and his big yellows eyes were looking at us.

"Guys," said Uzzy, his voice worryingly calm. "I think that maybe we should start backing away now."

"Do you think?" muttered Tia.

I tried to calm myself down. It couldn't be the reanimated body of a long-dead pharaoh (I was making an effort not to think the word "mummy") because these things don't exist. Then I remembered I was a time-traveller from the future, something else that technically did not exist.

I SCREAMED VERY LOUDLY AND RAN VERY FAST.

Refreshingly, for once, everyone screamed very loudly and ran very fast.

We **SCRAMBLED** past the room full of stuff, knocking lots of it on the floor as we stumbled over each other in the dark. We kept falling down in the corridor, and it felt like **AGES** until we reached the entrance room. We could hear the mummy (there you go, I said it) making its way through the mess in the big room, so we **SQUEEZED** through the front door into the valley, and ran back the way we had come from.

It was early afternoon when we got into the tomb, but now the sun was setting and the valley was very dark. Being outside felt a lot less safe than I thought it would have.

"**DID YOU SEE THAT?!?!?**" asked Hano.

"No, Hano," said Uzzy. "I just ran like a crazy antelope because I felt like some exercise. **OF COURSE I SAW IT!**"

"Wait until we tell the other guys we saw great-great-great granddad!" said Tia. She didn't look half as scared as I felt.

"That can't have been a real mummy," I said, still trying to convince myself there was another explanation. "I've read about grave robbers. That must have been a grave robber dressed as a mummy to scare people away."

They all looked at me as if I was a very unique type of idiot.

"Why would a grave robber go to all the trouble of dressing up as a mummy on the off chance someone came in?" asked Uzzy.

"Yeah, they could just take stuff and run away," added Hano.

"And how many grey people with shiny yellow eyes do you know, He-Ne-Re?" said Tia.

I was trying to remember how many grey people with shiny eyes I did know (zero at the first count) when we heard shouting. We all huddled together (I think we all thought it must be a horde of mummies coming to get us, which was perfectly plausible under the circumstances) when the noise became louder and closer.

It wasn't a horde of mummies, but Paser and the rest of the group. They were carrying torches and calling our names. He looked at us, looked at the open entrance to the tomb and the confusion of footsteps we left on the sandy floor.

We had been in enough trouble in the past few weeks, so I knew what to expect.

He was so cross he kept shouting at us all the way down the valley, across the river and into the palace.

I was so relieved at not being killed by a mummy (definitely close to the top of my Top 10 Things to Avoid list) that I didn't feel nearly as bad as I thought I should have.

7

The next morning I woke up feeling **GREAT**. I didn't know why, given my near escape from death, but hey.

I rolled over from Sobby and saw that Tia and Hano were already up. They also looked pretty smiley.

"Funny," said Hano. "I still remember the whole thing with the mummy, but now it feels fun instead of really scary."

"That's probably because now there's a mountain, a river, a city, a moat and two massive walls between the mummy and us," said Tia, laughing.

I would probably never break into a tomb again, of course, but there was no denying it had been more exciting than the afternoon I reorganized my bookshelf (that still had been very enjoyable, of course).

"Hano is right," I said. "It was super fun."

We went straight into geometry class after breakfast. I solved the problem we were given super-fast (working out the volume of three pyramids, easy), and used the rest of the time to try and remember the equation that would send me back home.

There's nothing like facing certain death (and the undead) to get the brain working. Unlike all the times I had tried to do this before, this time I seemed to remember everything that was written on the board back at school perfectly. By the end of the morning I got something that looked a lot like the problem Mr Borderman had written.

I waited until everyone had left the classroom (they were used to me staying behind to do extra work by now) and started to write the solution down.

This was a little bit less easy than remembering the question; I had to go back and forth a few times, and every time I got something wrong I had to start on a new papyrus (there's a reason we don't use papyrus and ink-dipped reeds in schools today, I guess).

I wasn't going to give up, and by the thirteenth or fourteenth papyrus, I was getting closer to something that felt right. The numbers and letters looked exactly like what I had done the first time – **THIS WAS IT!**

I painted the last stroke of the answer with my reed. **MY HANDS WERE SHAKING AND I COULD FEEL** ...

... NOTHING.

Nothing appeared in the air. No wind blew. No swirling vortex of space and time roared.

I checked the equation again. I could remember it perfectly now, and was sure it was right.

That was it. My only plan to escape the past and get back home. And it hadn't worked.

For the first time since I had appeared in Ancient Egypt, I had no idea what to do next.

I only realized I was crying when Tia put her hand on my shoulder.

"What's wrong He-Ne-Re?" she said. "I've never seen you cry before. Moan, YES, whinge, ALWAYS, but not cry."

"It's … nothing," I said. "It makes no sense – I don't think you would believe me if I told you."

"The only way you'll find out is if you tell me," she said.

So I did. It took me ages, but I explained everything: where (and when) I was from, what had happened to me before they found me in the desert, how I had been trying to find a way back home and what had just happened (or not happened, to be more precise) that made me so sad.

When I finished, surprisingly, she didn't laugh in my face.

"Well, that explains the TERRIBLE HAIR, the LUDICROUS CLOTHES and the RIDICULOUS NAME," she said. We both smiled a bit, even though I couldn't help to feel offended by the hair thing.

"I'm afraid you might be stuck with me for ever," I said.

"Nonsense," she said. "You can't give up after trying a single thing. You have to keep going. I can help; Hano can help too. I'm sure we'll find a way to conjure your magical time thingy."

A few moments ago I was incredibly sad, but now things seemed a bit better. It felt really good telling someone about it. It felt great, actually.

I picked up the papyrus with the equation and we went outside together to bother some hippos.

2ND YEAR OF THE REIGN OF SETI I.
4TH DAY OF THE 3RD MONTH OF HARVEST

One morning we got back from breakfast and found servants packing lots of stuff in our room.

Paser walked in and explained we were all going to join the pharaoh's royal hunt.

"**YESSS!**" cried Uzzy. "I've been waiting for this all year!"

"*I FINALLY GET TO TRY OUT MY NEW SPEAR!*" said Merry, and they ran off to get their hunting gear.

"I guess this is kind of a big deal," I said to Tia and she rolled her eyes.

"Kind of," she said. "If you like hunting and killing animals."

"The way I've been doing in hunting lessons, it's much more likely that the animals will be trying to kill me."

"Well, it doesn't matter," she said. "Father insists we all go every year, so we have to be there."

I cheered up a bit when Tia told me we weren't going to travel in chariots or camels. Finally some good news.

We went to the riverbank, where we boarded a **HUGE FANCY BOAT.** It was covered in gold, with lots of things built on to it: wooden rooms, small tents, a kitchen and even some statues.

All of Seti's court, priests, cooks, and hundreds of servants and guards were coming along too. They boarded other boats, and after a long time we all set off down the river.

Ancient Egyptian transportation kept surprising me. It turns out that travelling on the boat is even worse than travelling by chariot or camel. The whole thing bobbed very slowly on the water, and it made me feel **VERY SICK.** Just me, of course; everyone else seemed absolutely fine.

I didn't think the pharaoh would appreciate me vomiting on his beautiful golden boat, so I leant over the side to be sick in the river. **THAT WAS NOT A GREAT IDEA.** As soon as I lowered my head I saw lots of crocodiles following the boat in the water. The crocodiles saw me too, they looked at me with the same expression

Mumbles has when he sees a date ball.

I got back up and found a bucket to be sick in.

We travelled for days and days. One afternoon the boats stopped on the riverbank to give the rowers a rest, and I felt a little bit better. I sat up, and was getting used to not being totally horizontal for a change, when Master Heneb showed up.

"He-Ne-Re," he said, "I heard you weren't feeling too well. Travelling on the river is not for everyone."

"Thanks, Master," I said. "It's better now the boat has stopped."

"I have been thinking about the question you asked me, He-Ne-Re," he said.

"Which one?" I asked. I had asked Master Haneb a lot of questions. Yesterday I had asked him how to stop being violently sick every twenty minutes (he couldn't help with that one much).

"About whether someone could travel through time," he said.

I tried to sit up more straight. "And?" I said.

"If someone wanted to move back and forth in time, like you described," he said, "then perhaps when they do it matters as much as how they do it."

I stared at him blankly. He smiled.

"Do you remember how I explained to you that time

is a circle, and the same things happen over and over again, always at the same time?" he asked.

"I do. It's an interesting theory," I said, even though I thought it was **BONKERS.**

"That means certain things can only happen at specific times," he said. "We can only sow after the Nile has flooded, we can only work after the sun has risen or sleep after night arrives. If a person wants to journey through time as you describe, perhaps they can only do it at the right moment."

I was going to ask what that moment might be when the rowers started again and I was sick all over my sandals.

Later that night we moored and I stopped being sick. I went and found Tia and Hano.

"Tia, I need to speak to you," I said. "About my … you know … situation."

"I think that's something that Hano could help with too," she said. "After all, he's smarter than any of us."

I looked at Hano. "Fine, but you won't believe this."

I told him everything as simply and quickly as I could. He nodded along, and when I had finally finished said, "I do believe you."

"Really?" I said.

"Time is a funny thing," he said, "and you don't have to understand something to believe in it."

That made me feel better. I don't like keeping secrets from my friends, and it's not like anyone else would have believed them if they told.

I explained what Master Heneb had said to me.

"Mmmm…" Tia said. "I wonder what he meant."

"I don't think it's that complicated," said Hano. That was news to me.

"He said the *when* mattered as much as the *how*," Hano said. "Right?"

"Yes," I said.

"So let's say this equation is the *how…*"

"Yes," I said again, **EXASPERATED,** "but I've done it already and nothing has happened."

"Yes, but,'" Hano continued, "you didn't know about the *when*. The time you wrote it down was also important. So maybe you have to do it again at the exact same time you did it in the first place. Same hour, same day, same month."

I was going to say that was a ridiculous idea, but it wasn't any more ridiculous than being flung back **THREE THOUSAND YEARS** in time for writing some maths on a board, so I didn't.

"Thanks, Hano. It makes a weird sort of sense," I said. "It's worth giving it a go."

The next morning the three of us sat down (I kind of leant against some cushions) with some papyrus and a borrowed calendar to try and work out which day I had arrived. It wasn't easy, but after a while we worked it out.

THE DAY I ARRIVED

(ACCORDING TO PASER'S RECORDS)

HOUR	DAY	MONTH	SEASON

HOUR	DAY	MONTH	SEASON
?	?	?	?

**CAN YOU FIND OUT WHAT THE DATE IS BEFORE
HENRY AND HIS FRIENDS DO?**

THE ANCIENT EGYPTIAN CALENDAR

(USE THESE SYMBOLS TO SOLVE THE PUZZLE)

HOURS

HOURS BEFORE

SUN RISE

MIDDAY

SUNSET

HOURS AFTER

DAYS

1

2

3

AND SO ON UNTIL WE GET TO

10

20, ETC

MONTHS

1ST

2ND

3RD

4TH

SEASONS

FLOOD

SOWING

HARVEST

It turns out I had been in Ancient Egypt for almost a whole year.

"I can't tell if it feels like a lot longer or a lot less time," I said, "but that means…"

"… THAT IN EXACTLY THREE DAYS, YOU CAN GIVE IT A GO!" said Hano.

"Do you think that if I write the equation again at the right time it'll send me back?" I asked him.

"You'll only find out if you try," he said.

Tia was smiling. "I can't believe you've finally solved this," she said.

She gave me a hug. "This is it, Henry. In a few days you'll be back home."

I wasn't so sure, but they

seemed **SUPER CONFIDENT** that it was going to work this time, and that made me feel pretty good about it too.

There was a loud call from the deck; we had finally arrived at the hunting grounds.

The boats moored. Stepping out on to solid ground felt amazing (even though the ground wasn't that solid – it was mud and we were wearing sandals).

You know things have been bad when just standing still feels like a treat.

The land around us was very green and quite **JUNGLY.** We walked between the trees for a while until we got to a big clearing that had been cut by the guards.

People were putting up tents, making fires, sharpening spears and stringing bows.

"I wonder what sort of hunt we will go on first!" said Uzzy.

"I just hope we don't kill any crocodiles," said Tia. "They remind me of Sobby, with their big smiles and little pudgy feet."

"I bet it'll be monkeys," mumbled Hano.

Whatever it was that we would be hunting, it didn't matter too much to me – I'd be useless no matter what. So far in school I had been unable to hunt anything. Birds, lizards or toads, they all escaped or attacked me first. Even a particularly large spider bit my face before I had a chance to spear it.

Paser called for silence.

"CHILDREN, WE HAVE A SPECIAL TREAT FOR YOU ALL," he said, a big smile on his face. "We have decided you are ready to set off on your own. Master Tchay will lead you down the hunting trail and then return to the camp. You will stay behind for the night and come back tomorrow."

Master Tchay stepped forward. He did not have a big smile on his face, and looked even **BIGGER** and more **SCARY** out here in the jungle, covered in sweat and carrying all sorts of pointy and sharp things about him. **"LISTEN, YOU GAGGLE OF DIM BABOONS,"** he said. Charming as always. "You'll have to find water, hunt for food and navigate your own way back. You've been learning all of this for a long time, so it should be no trouble." He smiled nastily.

I was pretty sure one of the things I had learnt was that going into a jungle without any food or water was not the most ideal of situations.

During the last few months I had almost died in so many unexpected ways that I didn't feel any need to explore the more expected ways to die. The others clearly felt different, there were lots of **"YAYS!"** and **"HURRAHS!"** from everyone as we grabbed our things and followed Master Tchay out of the clearing.

The jungle was hot and humid, so in less than five minutes' walking we were completely drenched in sweat. We walked for **AGES** following a small creek between the trees, pushing vines and bushes out of the way. I had thought the desert was deadly, but it was a paradise of safety compared to the jungle. As we walked through I saw:

We finally left the jungle, walked past a huge pile of boulders and on to some grasslands. By the time the sun was setting we had arrived at the foothills of a range of huge rocky mountains.

Master Tchay told us to drop our stuff and sit down. **"OK, YOU PACK OF BOG LIZARDS,"** he said, with his usual politeness, "this is where I leave you. You're on your own now. Stay here until the morning and then you can start to make your way back. I hope you have been paying attention to the route or else…" He smiled a not-too-friendly smile. "You might not make it."

Uzzy looked super-confident, but then again you could tie Uzzy upside down on top of a pool filled with lava and sharks and he would look confident (the sharks probably wouldn't).

Despite the tiredness and hunger, I was also feeling quite confident about one thing. I was terrible at hunting, but I was very good at paying attention, and I remembered everything from our orienteering classes.

Since no one had any maps or phones to help find the way, we had to remember as many features of the landscape as we went along. That's just what I had done, and I was pretty sure I could find our way back when time came.

Master Tchay waved goodbye and left, running at a steady trot. He could have walked, of course, but he seemed quite intent with turning every activity into a workout. For all I know he probably slept doing crunches...

"All right," said Uzzy. "We have to make a fire, find food and build some sort of shelter."

"Hano and Kneb, you gather wood. Merry, Nebby and Dedu, you come with me to hunt. Tia, Neffy and He-Ne-Re, you make a shelter," he said, pointing at us.

"Wait a moment," said Tia. She didn't look too happy. **"WHO MADE YOU THE BOSS OF EVERYONE?"**

"I did," said Uzzy. "I'm the oldest, I'm the heir to the

throne and I am better at this stuff than any of you."

"No you're not," said Tia. If anyone else had argued with Uzzy like that they'd be lying on the floor by now, but she was the only person he seemed to treat as an equal (which meant he thought she was absolutely incredibly amazing).

"We should all go and hunt first," she said. "We can do the other stuff when we get back."

I hated to admit it, but Uzzy's plan seemed better. It was almost dark, and it made a lot more sense to split the tasks so we would be fed and ready for bed once it got dark. Still, I had no desire to take Uzzy's side on any argument (or to be on the other side of an argument with Tia).

Uzzy and Tia couldn't stand to be around each other after they had an argument, so we split in two groups. Uzzy and the rest of the kids went to the grasslands, looking for antelope. Tia, Hano and I went towards the mountains, where she was hoping to find a lake and catch some fish or something (I was hoping for a particularly sluggish gerbil).

We walked up the mountainside for a while. I climbed on a big rock to try and see if I could spot the lake, or anything small and easy to catch, like a coconut.

"There's a big hairy monkey there," I said.

"We're not killing a monkey," said Tia (which was good, both for the monkey and for me).

I kept looking.

"There's a snake under those rocks," I said.

"Too bony," said Hano.

"All right then. There's a goat climbing over there," I tried again.

"It's too far. We'll never be able to catch it," said Tia.

I had no intention of killing any of the animals I had spotted, but this not-too-helpful attitude was beginning to annoy me. Everyone was *TIRED, HUNGRY* and getting *VERY GRUMPY.*

"Well, Tia. If you think you can do better, why don't you find something instead?" I said.

She gave me a surly look, climbed on the rock and looked around.

"I've seen something!" she said, pointing at a cave behind us.

She didn't look very happy about it, and with my recent (and not-so-recent) track record of disaster I knew it could not be good news. I wasn't even that surprised when I saw an **ENORMOUS LION** come out of the cave.

"IT HAS SEEN US!" shouted Hano. During months of hunting class I hadn't even been able to hunt an insect. I was pretty sure hunting a lion was not the next step Paser had in mind for me. Hano and Tia must have felt the same, because, as soon as the lion **ROARED** at us, they jumped down from the rock and ran down the mountain as fast as they could.

After a brief moment (when I enjoyed the unusual feeling of not being the first person in a situation to run away from something in a blind panic) I also jumped from the rock, and ran away from the lion in a blind panic.

Walking up the mountain had been hard work, but running down was even harder.

The mountain was very steep, so the faster I went the less contact with the ground my feet made. Contact with the ground is quite an important part of running, and once my feet stopped touching anything I fell forward and **TUMBLED** face first into a pile of rocks.

Hitting the rocks **HURT A LOT**, but I hoped they would at least stop my mad tumbling.

They didn't.

The rocks came loose and joined the tumbling, all

of which was less than ideal. I rolled down the mountain in a blur of loose boulders, torn bushes, dirt and confused children. We all arrived at the foot of the mountain together in a small but very painful rockslide.

It wasn't all bad news, though. The lion had been put off by the whole thing and, instead of coming down to eat us, it retreated back into its cave.

TAKE THAT, LION.

We hobbled back to camp and found the others had been a little bit more successful in their hunting than us.

Uzzy and a couple of guys were skinning a whole gazelle next to a fire. Some other kids had built a shelter using some large palm leaves and were carrying water in some skins.

All seemed to be fine, except for the fact Tia, Hano and I hadn't really done much to help, and I didn't like feeling useless.

"I don't want to wait until morning to go back," said Uzzy. "Let's go as soon as we finish eating."

Tia sighed. "Why would we do that?"

"Because I want to show them we can do things better and faster than what they expect us to."

Tia and Hano looked at each other.

"I'm not sure that's a great idea," I said, trying to sound reasonable. After all, Uzzy and I had been getting on OK lately. He hadn't tried to kill me for weeks. "If we wake early and wait until the sun comes out, we can work out where we are and which direction to take. It makes no sense to leave now."

"**PAH**," said Uzzy. "We don't need to look at any sun or stars. I know where we are."

I was hurt, hungry and too tired to continue trying to make my point politely.

"No, you don't know where we are, Uzzy," I said. "You have no idea."

"I do," he said. "We just go through that gap in the trees over there and take that path straight back through the jungle."

"That's completely wrong. There are dozens of gaps in that jungle and dozens of paths and all of them look the same," I said. "Wait until the morning and we'll know the direction we are meant to follow."

"**YOU'RE JUST SCARED!**" he shouted. "**SCARED AND LAZY!**"

"**ALL YOU KNOW IS HOW TO HIT STUFF!**" I shouted back. "**ARE YOU GOING TO WRESTLE YOUR WAY BACK?**"

Perhaps bringing wrestling into the discussion wasn't the best idea. Uzzy went very red and jumped on top of me. I had improved a little bit on our

Arts of War classes (little Kammy barely made me cry any more), and that was enough to prevent my immediate death.

The other guys ran over and pulled us apart. When Tia saw that Uzzy and I had calmed down a bit (I did most of the calming down) she spoke:

"Look," she said. "I think we should vote on this. Everyone who thinks that Uzzy is right and we should leave now, raise their hand."

Uzzy raised his hand. No one else did.

"OK..." said Tia. "Who thinks Henry is right and we should wait until morning?"

Everyone raised their hands, except Uzzy of course. I almost felt sorry for him, but I didn't really.

Despite pretending to be fine, Uzzy was clearly as tired as the rest of us. He didn't try to talk us into leaving again.

After dinner we all settled down to sleep.

Despite being worried about all the danger we were in (from hyenas, cheetahs, crocodiles, unusually large rats, take your pick) I was also super excited. In two days I would be able to get back home again.

I had put the papyrus with the equation and my writing stuff in a little leather bag, and I checked for the millionth time that it was still tied to my kilt. I was running over what I would have to do when the right time came (for the MILLIONTH time) when I fell asleep.

We woke up and made breakfast (well, divvied up the cold leftovers of last night's roast). The sun was making its way from behind the jungle, which was good news. It confirmed that the trees were on the east, and that we should go that way.

"Look," I said, pointing at the sun, "the sun's in the east. The river is east too, so we should keep following that direction when we go through the jungle."

I had no intention of starting last night's argument again, but Uzzy wouldn't be Uzzy if he let someone else be right.

"That's it?" he snorted. "And what do we do when we get into the jungle and can't see the sun? Hadn't thought of that, had you?"

"I have," I said. "We'll still have the daylight. I made a point of remembering lots of landmarks on our way here, so once we're in I can find the way."

"YOU THINK YOU KNOW EVERYTHING!"

he said. He turned to the others and shouted, "You're not going to follow this **IMBECILE**, are you?"

"That imbecile seems to have a much better idea of how to get us back than this imbecile," said Tia. She picked her things up and walked over to me. So did Hano. And then the rest of the kids followed.

Uzzy stood there, **FUMING.** After a while he gave up sulking and came over too.

We spent most of the morning making our way back. The jungle was **DARK** and **THICK**, so it was really hard to know what direction we were going, but I kept looking out for some of the places we had seen yesterday, and I knew we were heading the right way.

Every time I stopped to try and figure out which way to go next, Uzzy would complain and try to rush us, but everyone ignored him.

It wasn't easy. At one point the canopy was so thick we couldn't see the sun at all and we almost got lost. I was about to give up when I noticed a huge line of termites making their way to our left and remembered we had walked past some big termite mounds on the previous day.

We followed the termites and soon were back on track.

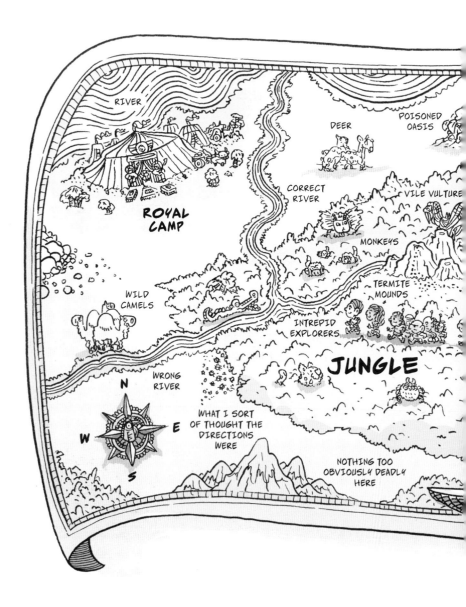

RIVER

DEER

POISONED OASIS

CORRECT RIVER

VILE VULTURE

ROYAL CAMP

MONKEYS

TERMITE MOUNDS

WILD CAMELS

INTREPID EXPLORERS

JUNGLE

WRONG RIVER

N
W   E
S

WHAT I SORT OF THOUGHT THE DIRECTIONS WERE

NOTHING TOO OBVIOUSLY DEADLY HERE

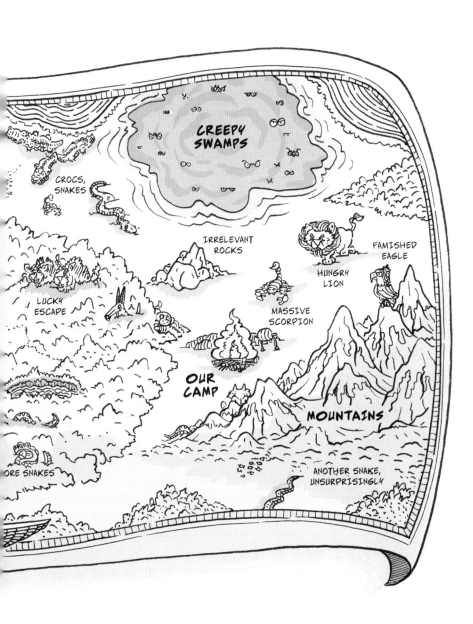

A little later we got to the little creek and walked alongside it until it branched into two smaller streams. I was trying to figure out which one to follow when we heard **LOUD STOMPING** and cracking noises coming through the trees in front of us.

We got our hunting gear out and scrambled to hide behind the trees. It sounded like a huge animal was rampaging through the forest, which is never ideal if you're trying to make your way back home. The noise grew louder. Uzzy lifted his spear, Tia and Nebby had their bows pulled and even I had a slingshot ready to go.

9

...STILL THE SAME DAY

A tangle of branches parted right in front of us, and a man tripped forward. It was one of the pharaoh's guards, I remembered him from the boat, and his name was Mahu. He was covered in cuts, filthy with sweat and dirt, and didn't look too well.

"Princes, princess..." he **GASPED.** "I'm very sorry."

"What happened?" asked Uzzy.

"The Royal Camp," said Mahu. "It was attacked in the night. River pirates. They took us by surprise, tied us all up and are robbing all of your father's treasure."

That didn't sound very good.

"I managed to escape and came here to find you," he said. "We need to get as far away from the camp as we can!"

Uzzy looked at him with an odd expression. It was the same face Uzzy's dad had made when we got into all that trouble in the market.

"You have done well to warn us, Mahu," he said, "but there's no way we will abandon our parents and teachers in the hands of some dirty pirates."

"THAT'S RIGHT!" I said firmly. **"NO WAY! WAIT, WHAT DO YOU MEAN, NO WAY?"**

Uzzy gave me that same level look. "I mean," he said, "that we are going to save them all ... or die trying."

I didn't want to abandon anyone, but pirates don't have the best of reputations when it comes to keeping people alive. I did quite enjoy the idea of staying alive.

"We'll get back to the camp and find a way to free everyone," Uzzy said.

"It's impossible," said Mahu. "If a regiment of Royal Guards were not strong enough to stop the pirates, there's no way a few kids can. With all due respect, your royal brilliance."

"Well, then," said Uzzy, looking thoughtful. "If we are not strong enough to defeat them, then we will have to be clever enough to do it."

He looked straight at me when he said it.

I felt all warm and happy. For a second. Then I felt worried. The guard was right; there was no way we could defeat a band of murderous pirates on our own.

The other guys also seemed pretty unsure about the whole thing. Uzzy was the only one that thought this was a good idea. He looked at everyone.

"I know this sounds crazy, but we can do it," he said. "We defeated an **ANGRY MOB, RAVENOUS HIPPOS** and even **A MUMMY.** He-Ne-Re, you're the **WEAKEST** of us. The **SMALLEST,** the **PUNIEST,** the **WHINGIEST** ,..."

"Er... Thanks a lot?" I muttered.

"... and in the last few hours you got everyone safely through the jungle without breaking a sweat."

That wasn't necessarily

true, I was sweating loads and I'm pretty sure there were weaker kids around here somewhere, but I appreciated the sentiment.

"With He-Ne-Re's help, we will free our parents," he said. "Trust me."

I still didn't like the idea of choosing to go and fight a band of bloodthirsty pirates loaded with weapons (it's a well-known fact all pirates have a thirst for blood, which is odd because blood is very salty), but when Uzzy put it like that it really felt like we could do it.

Mahu was too hurt and tired to argue with us or to walk any further. He tried to come along,

but couldn't walk and was too heavy for us to carry, so we gave him some water and the leftovers from the roast gazelle, and we promised we'd be back to get him once we had freed everyone.

We continued to make our way through the forest. It was much easier going now; the soldier had trampled over everything on his run towards us, so we could see which way to go. A few more hours' walking and we arrived at the edge of the clearing around the Royal Camp and hid behind some trees to take a look at the state of things.

THINGS DID NOT LOOK GOOD.

The whole place was surrounded by SCARY-LOOKING people. They were all really different: one was a big beardy man in a blue tunic, another had red hair and was completely covered in tattoos, a really strong woman was bumping the end of a massive iron staff on the floor in a bored sort of way, whilst a guy in a bronze helmet and a leather skirt sharpened a sword.

Inside the camp things were even worse – lots of things had been set on fire, and huge columns of smoke were rolling towards the sky. We could see the pharaoh and his men sitting on the floor in the middle of the tents that were still left. Their arms and legs were tied together with thick rope, their clothes were torn and they were covered in bruises.

A very short man wearing a furry coat walked to the middle of the camp and called to all the pirates.

"COMRADES!" he said. "This morning we have captured the mighty pharaoh Seti. Tomorrow we will present him as a gift to the gods."

That didn't sound too bad. Perhaps they were going to wrap the pharaoh nicely with a bow and put him under a tree, with a little card saying, "DEAR GODS, I HOPE YOU LIKE THIS PHARAOH. XXX, PIRATE CHIEF."

189

"LET'S BUILD A FIRE, AND WHEN THE SUN RISES
AGAIN, WE SHALL BURN ALL THESE PEOPLE AND
SEND THEM AS OFFERINGS TO HEAVEN!" he yelled.
He was surprisingly loud for such a small person.

All the pirates raised their weapons and howled. It
was not a nice sound.

We moved back into the jungle until we were sure no one would hear us.

"This is way worse than I thought" said Uzzy. "Not only are they pirates, they're also **TOTAL LUNATICS.** I was hoping they'd let our parents go once they took all the treasure."

Tia was staring at him very hard. I knew by now that was her thinking face.

"Yes, they're fanatics," she said, "but maybe that's not a bad thing."

"How is the fact they want to burn everyone we know not a bad thing?" asked Hano, always one to focus on the positive.

"Well," said Tia. "They fear their gods so much they are prepared to sacrifice the king to them, right?"

"Yes?" said Uzzy.

"So, that means they'll do anything their gods will tell them to do, right?"

"Oh…" I said. "I see."

"I don't," said Uzzy. No surprise there.

"If we find a way to convince them we are their gods, we can tell them to let our parents go," finished Tia.

Uzzy stared.

"It's never going to work," he said. "How are we going to convince anyone we're gods? You and I could pass, Tia, but look at Merry and He-Ne-Re… No offence."

I was so astonished Uzzy had said "no offence" that I didn't even get offended.

"I think there's a way," I said. "We just need some serious arts and crafts skills, and luckily for you all, I am excellent at arts and crafts."

Clearly no one knew what arts and crafts meant, but they were still waiting for me to finish explaining the plan.

"We'll use what we have – papyrus, ink, wood, feathers and whatever else we can find to make some big animal masks," I said. "Lots of your gods look like animals, right?"

"Yes," said Tia. "But we're too small to look like gods."

"That's true," I said, "but perhaps we could be on top of something. There were horses on the boats with us. If they are still in the camp we could steal some and ride. We brought so many that no one would notice if a few went missing."

Uzzy's smile had returned. "You're crazy. But it's worth a try. I'll get into the camp with Hano and steal some horses, you guys get going with the masks."

I gave him a thumbs up. He looked at my hand and, after a second, closed his fist awkwardly, pulled his thumb up and gave me one back.

HOW TO LOOK LIKE AN EGYPTIAN GOD

(ON A SMALL OR NON-EXISTENT BUDGET)

MAKING THE COSTUMES WAS SURPRISINGLY FUN, DESPITE THE FACT WE WERE IN A MASSIVE HURRY AND TRYING TO PREVENT A TERRIBLE CATASTROPHE. HERE'S HOW WE GOT ONE OF THE MASKS DONE:

SMALL LEAVES

HANO KNEW HOW TO GET ALL SORTS OF COLOURS FROM MASHING FRUITS AND LEAVES (YOU CAN ALSO GET A NASTY BURN, AS I FOUND OUT...)

BIG LEAVES

ATTACHING THE LEAVES TO ONE ANOTHER WAS A LOT LESS SIMPLE THAN IT SEEMED AT FIRST.

194

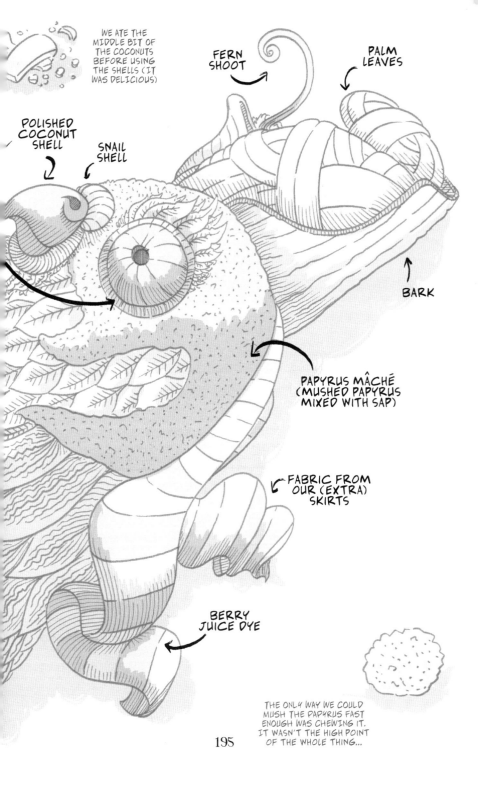

WE ATE THE MIDDLE BIT OF THE COCONUTS BEFORE USING THE SHELLS (IT WAS DELICIOUS)

FERN SHOOT

PALM LEAVES

POLISHED COCONUT SHELL

SNAIL SHELL

BARK

PAPYRUS MÂCHÉ (MUSHED PAPYRUS MIXED WITH SAP)

FABRIC FROM OUR (EXTRA) SKIRTS

BERRY JUICE DYE

THE ONLY WAY WE COULD MUSH THE PAPYRUS FAST ENOUGH WAS CHEWING IT. IT WASN'T THE HIGH POINT OF THE WHOLE THING...

195

Uzzy and Hano came back with the horse as we were finishing the masks.

"These masks look **GREAT,**" said Uzzy. "Very impressive." He glanced at the sky. "We need to get going. The sun's about to rise and they'll start the bonfire soon."

"Let's divvy up the masks," said Tia.

"Horus is the best, so obviously I get him," said Uzzy.

196

"**I WANT SEKHMET!**" said Tia, grabbing an angry looking lioness's head.

Nebby got the jackal head of Anubis, Neffy was Bastet (a cat), Merry was Sobek (a crocodile) and so on. I was left with Thoth, the chap with the head of a stork. He wasn't too scary, but the Egyptians thought he had invented writing, so that was cool with me.

197

People say the pen is mightier than the sword anyway (not that I had a pen or a sword, just some writing reeds and a slingshot).

I thought we all looked **PRETTY SCARY**, which, for me at least, was a first.

"Thanks for this, Henry," said Tia.

I shrugged, as if it was nothing. "Let's go scare some pirates pantless," I said, and everyone cheered.

But then I realized something. Something rather important.

We had taken almost two days to get back to the camp and make our costumes, so by the time the sun rose it would be ... exactly the right time for me to try and get back home.

I didn't want to let my Egyptian friends down, but I also didn't want to be stuck here for ever. I didn't know what to do.

I thought about how sad my mum and dad (and probably Rosie, though I wouldn't bet on it) would be if I didn't come back. That made me **INCREDIBLY SAD** too. It also made me realize that's how my friends right there and then felt about their families being taken hostage.

Once I understood that, I had no real choice to make. I had to stay and help them, and if I had to wait another year to go back, that would be it.

"Henry?" said Uzzy. "Are you coming?"

I nodded.

I got my hunting weapons and climbed on to the horse. It felt more solid and less tall than the camels. So far so good.

"Follow me slowly," said Uzzy. "We'll wait until they are about to light the bonfire and then we ride in. Once you get going, don't stop!"

It was impossible to see much wearing a huge fake animal head whilst riding a horse in the jungle as the rising sun shone straight into our eyes, but perhaps, given we were probably riding to our doom, that was a good thing.

We got to the edge of the forest just as the little pirate chap walked towards a massive pile of wood that had been gathered around the people who were on the ground, still tied up. We couldn't hear what the pirate leader was saying, but when he lifted the torch above his head Uzzy kicked his horse and yelled:

Our horses **GALLOPED** behind his. I held on to mine with one hand and to the giant stork mask with the other. I was also yelling very loudly, but more out of sheer **TERROR** than from any desire to scare the pirates.

My expectations for the attack weren't too high. I thought we might scare them for a minute or two before they realized we were just some kids wearing

masks. But it turns out that the pirates were a very superstitious and gullible bunch after all, and our costumes worked better than we could·have hoped for.

The sun rising through the smoke coming out of the burning tents made everything look fuzzy and shiny. It was hard to see much, what with me trying to hold on to the horse and all the **SCREAMING** and **SHOUTING**, but I could see how scared the pirates were.

The big pirate with the red hair threw down his spear on the floor, turned around, tripped over himself and finally managed to **SCRAMBLE** out of the camp on all fours.

A man with a huge moustache dropped his swords and started crying like a baby.

A woman wearing chain mail ran surprisingly fast, pushing lots of other pirates out of the way as she went.

The pirate chief's eye opened so wide that I thought they would pop out of his head and float off. It was quite nice to see a look of **TOTAL TERROR** in someone else's face and not just mine, but I was too busy trying not to die to enjoy it.

The little bald man opened his mouth to scream, but made no sound. When he started running away, the few pirates that were still looking after the prisoners dropped everything and ran off too.

They kept running until they reached the river, then hopped into their boat and rowed away as fast as they could.

We couldn't believe it –

OUR PLAN HAD WORKED!

Neither, for that matter, could all the grown-ups that had been captured by the pirates.

We dismounted (I fell, of course), took our masks off and started untying everyone. Uzzy and Tia found their parents, and so did Hano and all the other guys. There were lots of tears and hugs all around.

"I don't quite understand how, but you saved us all," said the pharaoh. "The sun hasn't risen in the sky yet, but you have brought light into our day."

Did Seti just say "the sun hasn't risen in the sky yet"?

The whole thing had happened so quickly that the sun had barely finished rising. I STILL HAD TIME TO TRY AND GET BACK HOME! HA!

I reached for the little bag with the papyrus that was tied around my waist, ready to scribble down the equation – but it wasn't there.

It must have fallen off during our attack.

I looked around for it on the ground, but there was such a mess of people, horses and dust that I couldn't see anything. I don't know how long I spent looking for it around the camp, but when I looked up again the sun had already moved high up into the sky.

The time to get back home had come and gone.

I felt **COMPLETELY BROKEN**. I was so tired and sad I barely looked up when a big shadow appeared in front of me. It was Paser.

"He-Ne-Re! I'm so glad you're not harmed!" he said, picking me up. "You children were **AMAZING**. I can't tell you how worried we were when the pirates trapped us."

Seti was there too. He coughed. Everyone stopped talking and looked at him.

"Children," he said, "never, in our noble history, has anyone done what you have done today. We would like to apologize for having failed to protect you and thank you for saving our lives. Anything that you want is yours."

Seti wasn't the sort of person who displays a lot of emotion (I think it comes with the pharaoh job), but he had a great big grin on his face now. He beckoned his kids over and hugged them, even Uzzy looked a little bit teary.

Everyone started moving back towards the river path. They couldn't wait to go back to Waset. Back to their home. I just stood there; it was probably the longest I had been silent in my whole life (if you don't count sleeping).

Tia, Hano and Uzzy came over.

"What happened He-Ne-Re," Tia asked. "Are you hurt?"

"No," I mumbled, "it's just that this morning was the time, you know? The right time for me to try and get back home, and now it's gone."

Hano and Tia suddenly looked quite sad too.

"Of course," said Hano. "It had to be at sunrise. I'm so sorry, He-Ne-Re."

"I don't get it," said Uzzy. "What on earth are the three of you talking about?"

"It's not a simple story," said Tia, "and I'll explain it to you properly later. The short version is He-Ne-Re got sent here from the future through some kind of magic, and the only time he could try to get back was today."

"Today?" asked Uzzy, looking a bit confused.

"Yes," I said. "Not just today, but just a moment ago. At the first hour after sunset, the second day of the first month of Flooding."

Uzzy thought for a while. He usually has to. Then he smiled. "You idiot," he said.

I thought we had turned a corner in our relationship in the last few days, so that felt very insensitive.

"That's tomorrow," he said.

"No, it's not," I said. "We all know the calendar. Yesterday was the last day of the season of Harvest."

"No, it wasn't!" said Uzzy. "Remember, Master Haneb taught us how they sometimes add an extra day to the end of each month of the season to make the right number of days in a year. That extra day was yesterday."

I couldn't believe I still had a chance! I also couldn't believe Uzzy had been paying attention in class.

Hano, Tia and Uzzy helped me look for my bag around the camp. It took almost a whole day, but eventually Hano found it on the clearing in the jungle where we had made the masks.

We followed the others back to the boats, but it was dark now and we would only set off in the morning. Instead of going to their hammocks, Tia and Hano came over to where I was sitting. After a bit Uzzy shuffled over too. The four of us just sat there, looking at the stars reflected on the river.

"What's it like where you come from, He-Ne-Re?" Uzzy asked.

"It's really different in lots of ways – our chariots don't need horses, we have little things with moving pictures inside we play with, and we don't really keep hippos," I said. "But in other ways it's pretty much the same. Me and my friends play together like we do here, we also go to school every day too. Actually, every kid in my country goes to school every day."

"EVERY KID?!" asked Hano. "That's amazing."

"Yup, it is," I said. "What is even more amazing is that we don't have onions for breakfast. We have awesome things like chocolate cereal, pancakes and bacon."

"What's wrong with onions?" asked Tia.

"If I get started we will be here all night," I said.

It turned out we did stay there all night. We were still chatting when the sun began to rise. Everyone became very quiet, I got my things out and started to write the numbers down again. I don't know why, but I didn't want to look at my friends.

Uzzy came forward and hugged me. REALLY HARD. Turns out there wasn't much difference between wrestling Uzzy and being hugged by Uzzy.

Then Tia hugged me too, and so did Hano. I felt really happy and really sad at the same time. It's an odd way to feel, but not the worse. Tia squeezed something sharp into my hand.

"This is one of Sobby's teeth that broke off. I keep it for luck," she said. "Remember us, OK?"

I tried to say something, but was so choked up that no sound came out.

I sat down and wrote until I had almost finished the equation.

The last number was eight.

As I closed the loop in the middle, I heard the same weird noise I had heard a long time ago, back in my classroom in England. A little black dot appeared, floating in the air, and grew until it became a **HUGE BLACK AND WHITE SPIRAL.**

It looked as wild and scary as it had done the first time I saw it, but I had fought crocodiles, mummies and pirates since then. A little rip in space and time was not going to frighten me. I jumped right into it,

NOT SURE WHEN OR WHERE AGAIN

I woke up in a bright room full of people. I was lying on the floor and a man was leaning towards me.

"Henry," he said. It was a familiar voice. "Are you all right?"

The man's face got closer. It was Mr Borderman, my year six teacher. In England. In the future (which was now the present).

I HAD MADE IT BACK!

"Mr Borderman?" I said. "What year is this?"

"I think he is concussed," he said to Ryan and Evie, who were looking at me with worried faces.

"It's 2019, Henry. It's the first day of term," he said. "You were working on an equation on the board, something odd happened and you passed out. Can you

 222

count how many fingers I'm holding up?" He held up three fingers.

"Three?" I said.

"Very good," he said. "If you can manage to stand, let's go to the office and see what we can do to make you feel better."

I felt fine, but I didn't understand how this could still be the same moment I had left. I had spent almost a year in Ancient Egypt.

Or…

Maybe I hadn't been in Ancient Egypt all.

Perhaps I slipped, bumped my head and had dreamed the whole thing. Which was odd, because it had felt really real.

I sat in the school office waiting for Mr Borderman, who had gone to let my parents in.

I felt something uncomfortable poking me in my pocket, so I took it out.

It was a tooth.

A CROCODILE TOOTH!

I looked at my knee. The big scar I got from Kammy's spear was still there.

I HADN'T DREAMED THE WHOLE THING!

There was my diary, with everything I had done during my time in Waset in it. There was no way I could have written all of that if all I had done was lie unconscious on the classroom floor for a few minutes!

The door to the office opened, but it wasn't Mr Borderman or the school nurse. It was my mum and dad. They ran towards me and gave me big hug.

"Are you OK?" they asked. "Mr Boderman called us. He said you fell down and hit your head. Do you need to go to hospital?"

I held them very tight and I did not let go.

"It's nothing," I said (and compared to everything I had gone through, it really was nothing). "I'm so happy to see you."

"Er…" said my dad, "I think he does need to see a doctor, Ann."

I felt a hard kick on my shin and looked down. It was my little sister, Rosie. She jumped up, squeezed me really hard around the neck and gave me a big sloppy kiss.

Then she stole Sobby's tooth from my pocket, and ran off.

THE END
OR IS IT?

THE **BATTLE** OF THE

HUNTING GROUNDS

HENRY'S GUIDE TO SURVIVING LIFE IN ANCIENT EGYPT

IF THERE'S ONE THING I WISH I'D HAD WHEN I GOT SENT BACK IN TIME, IT'S A RELIABLE GUIDE BOOK. THERE AREN'T MANY TIME-TRAVELLING GUIDES IN THE LIBRARY, SO I DECIDED TO MAKE ONE.

YOU NEVER KNOW WHEN YOU TOO MIGHT MESS UP YOUR MATHS IN CLASS AND GET SENT BACK TO THE PAST, SO BEST KEEP THIS IN YOUR POCKET AT ALL TIMES...

RAMSES II
(NOT SUCH A TURNIP AFTER ALL)

WHEN YOU TRAVEL BACK IN TIME IT'S NOT JUST WHAT YOU KNOW THAT MATTERS, BUT WHO YOU KNOW. ALTHOUGH LIZZY WAS A NIGHTMARE WHEN WE FIRST MET, HE TURNED OUT TO BE OK IN THE END.

ONCE I WAS BACK TO MY OWN TIME, I LOOKED HIM UP AND FOUND THAT HE HAD BECOME A PHARAOH (I GUESS THAT MAKES SENSE WHAT WITH HIS DAD BEING A PHARAOH AND ALL THAT). AND IT TURNED OUT THAT LIZZY WAS REALLY GOOD AT THE JOB.

HE CHANGED HIS NAME TO RAMSES II (NEW PHARAOHS ALWAYS HAD TO CHOOSE A NEW NAME, I THINK I WOULD HAVE CHOSEN OLIVER OR COLIN) AND, AS WELL AS DOING WELL AT ALL THE FIGHTING AND WARS AND ALL THE OTHER THINGS I KNEW HE'D BE GOOD AT, HE WAS ALSO A GREAT ADMINISTRATOR, JUDGE AND THE STUFF THAT NEEDS MORE, ER, BRAINS. PEOPLE CALLED HIM "RAMSES THE GREAT" AND TODAY HE IS STILL CONSIDERED ONE OF THE GREATEST RULERS OF ALL TIME.

EVEN MORE SURPRISINGLY FOR SOMEONE WHO SPENT HIS LIFE FIGHTING, RIDING WILD ANIMALS AND SWINGING LARGE WEAPONS, LIZZY LIVED TO BE 90 YEARS OLD. NOT THAT MANY PEOPLE GET TO BE THIS OLD NOWADAYS, LET ALONE 3000 YEARS AGO, SO GOOD ON HIM.

I SORT OF MISS HIM SOMETIMES.

THE
GODs
OF
ANCIENT EGYPT

PEOPLE WERE QUITE SERIOUS ABOUT THEIR RELIGION IN ANCIENT EGYPT, SO KNOWING SOMETHING ABOUT THEIR GODS WILL GIVE YOU AN EASY TOPIC FOR CONVERSATION (A BIT LIKE TALKING ABOUT FOOTBALL OR THE WEATHER NOWADAYS). EGYPTIAN GODS WERE ALMOST AS CONFUSING (AND NUMEROUS) AS EGYPTIAN HIEROGLYPHS; HERE ARE A FEW OF THE MOST POPULAR:

OSIRIS

WAS THE KING OF EVERYTHING, GODS AND PEOPLE, UNTIL HIS BROTHER SETH KILLED HIM. BEING DEAD DIDN'T STOP OSIRIS FROM BEING BOSSY, SO HE BECAME THE KING OF THE DEAD INSTEAD. LOOKED LIKE AN AVERAGE PHARAOH, EXCEPT HE WAS VERY GREEN.

ANUBIS

THE TOP DOG OF EGYPTIAN GODS, EXCEPT HE WAS NOT A DOG AND WASN'T ANYONE'S BOSS, SO PERHAPS NOT THE BEST ANALOGY. WHEN OSIRIS DIED, ANUBIS WRAPPED HIM IN LINEN AND SORT OF INVENTED MUMMIES. WORKED IN THE UNDERWORLD.

ISIS

OSIRIS' WIFE AND ER... SISTER (IT
HAPPENED A LOT WITH EGYPTIAN
GODS). EGYPTIANS BELIEVED
THE NILE FLOODING WAS CAUSED
BY HER TEARS, WHAT WITH HER
BEING UPSET BY HER HUSBAND
BEING DEAD AND ALL THAT.

SEKHMET

THE NOT SO CHEERY GODDESS
OF BATTLE AND WRECKING
THINGS. SHE ONCE GOT SO
MAD SHE STARTED KILLING
EVERYONE IN SIGHT AND ONLY
STOPPED WHEN SOMEONE MADE
HER DRUNK AND SHE FELL ASLEEP.

HORUS

OSIRIS AND ISIS' KID (AND NEPHEW
TOO, RIGHT?) ALTHOUGH BOTH
HIS PARENTS LOOKED HUMAN,
HORUS HAD A MASSIVE FALCON'S
HEAD; I NEVER FOUND OUT IF HE
CAME OUT OF AN EGG OR NOT.
AFTER HIS DAD RETIRED HE
FOUGHT HIS UNCLE AND
BECAME KING OF THE GODS.

SOBEK

UNLIKE LOVELY SOBBY, SOBEK
WAS NOT THE FRIENDLIEST OF
DEITIES. WHAT MADE HIM BAD
COMPANY AT DINNER PARTIES
ALSO MADE HIM GREAT AS A
FIGHTER AND GUARD, SO HE
PROTECTED THE OTHER GODS
WHEN THEY NEEDED IT.

HOW TO WRITE IN HIEROGLYPHS

READING AND WRITING IN ANCIENT EGYPT WAS WAY HARDER THAN IT IS TODAY. INSTEAD OF A SIMPLE ALPHABET WHERE WORDS COMBINE TO MAKE SOUNDS, THE ANCIENT EGYPTIANS USED THOUSANDS OF SYMBOLS, SOME OF WHICH REPRESENTED WHOLE WORDS, WHILE OTHERS REPRESENTED CERTAIN SOUNDS OR EVEN COMBINATIONS OF SOUNDS. I WON'T SHOW YOU THE LOT HERE, BUT HERE ARE SOME BASIC SYMBOLS FOR THE SOUNDS OF WORDS THAT MIGHT HELP YOU WRITE 'PLEASE DON'T KILL ME, I COME FROM THE FUTURE' IN THE UNLIKELY (BUT NOT IMPOSSIBLE, AS WE FOUND OUT) EVENT OF YOUR ACCIDENTAL TRANSPORTATION TO THE PAST.

SEE IF YOU CAN WRITE YOUR NAME USING THE SYMBOLS ABOVE.
HENRY (WELL, HE-NE-RE OF SU-WA-RD) IS WRITTEN LIKE THIS:

HENRY's TOP 10

LIFE IN ANCIENT EGYPT ISN'T ALL BAD, SO IF YOU MANAGE TO
SURVIVE FOR LONG ENOUGH TRY AND HAVE SOME FUN.
HERE ARE THE THINGS I ENJOYED THE MOST:

- TIA, HANO, LIZZY AND THE GUYS

- FRIENDLY CROCODILES
(NEVER APPROACH ONE WITHOUT ASKING THE OWNER FIRST)

- CANDIED DATES

- LEARNING HOW TO WRAP A MUMMY

- A RELAXED APPROACH TO SCHOOL ATTIRE

- SWIMMING IN THE POND
(ALWAYS UNDER ADULT SUPERVISION, OF COURSE)

- MASTER HANEB AND HIS CRAZY THEORIES

- THE DESERT SKY AT NIGHT

- SLEEPING IN A BIG ROOM WITH ALL MY FRIENDS

- SAVING THE PHARAOH AND ALL HIS COURT
(I WON'T USE THE WORD "HERO", BUT IT WAS MENTIONED..)

HENRY's
BOTTOM 10

THERE WERE QUITE A FEW THINGS I DIDN'T LIKE TOO.
WHEN OVER THERE I WOULD TRY AND AVOID:

- ONIONS

- BEER

- CAMELS

- BLOODTHIRSTY PIRATES

- ANGRY BABOONS

- ANGRY TODDLERS

- SHARP WEAPONS

- ANGRY TODDLERS <u>WITH</u> SHARP WEAPONS

- MUMMIES THAT WON'T STAY DEAD

- ONIONS, AGAIN, BECAUSE THEY
  WERE EVERYWHERE

ACKNOWLEDGEMENTS

I spend most of my days in a tiny shed writing and drawing books, but that doesn't mean I make the books on my own. I don't get a chance to say thank you to people nearly as much as I should, and this feels like a good place to start. So, I'd like to thank:

Paul, for encouraging me to turn some terrible comic book ideas into a hopefully not so terrible book; Alison and Zoë who were there at the beginning; Sam and Fiz, for believing it was something worth making; and, specially, Gen and Jamie, who came along all the way and made the book funnier and more beautiful than I could have expected it to be.

A lot of the delight that I feel in writing for children comes from being around delightful children. My kids, Tom and Billie, and their friends have provided inspiration, laughs and a huge amount of noise. They haven't provided much sleep so far, but that's OK.

No one has had to listen to more terrible ideas, dreary puns and half-baked plot lines than my wife, Ana. Thank you for more than I can fit on a page.

I'm sure I have forgotten someone. Sorry … it'll come back to me as soon as the book goes to print.

HAIR

MORE
HAIR

EYEBROWS →
(ALSO HAIR)

WORK
TOOLS

TINY BIT NOT
COVERED IN HAIR

BEARD
(UNSURPRISINGLY
HAIR)

Thiago de Moraes writes and illustrates all sorts of books, which he makes in a tiny shed at the bottom of his garden.

One of these books, *Myth Atlas*, is a guide to many worlds of myths and legends (including the Ancient Egyptians') and has been published in 19 countries, with surprisingly few complaints so far.

He is 90% beard, dangerously fond of bacon and lives in England with his wife, kids and a pet tortoise called Nibbles.